AT LAST, A CLUE . . .

Delia ran out of the room and out of the library, standing for a moment at the top of the steps, wanting to roar back at the stone lions before her. She seethed with excitement during the ride downtown. Flinging a fifty dollar bill at the astonished cab driver, she raced into the medical examiner's office.

"I'm the Viscountess Ross-Merlani," she said to the receptionist. "Please ask Dr. Elliot if he might spare me a moment."

In his office, Delia took Daniel's face between her two hands and kissed him deeply. She felt his surprise, momentary rebellion, and final surrender: Daniel folded his arms about her.

Delia looked up at him as Daniel pushed the wet hair off her face, looking deeply into her eyes. "I know how Magda died . . . how she was murdered," she said. "I may even know by whom."

Daniel nodded and tightened his arms around her. And he knew absolutely, as he had not known anything in his life before, that he would never let this woman walk out of his life again.

A DELIA ROSS-MERLANI MYSTERY

BORN
TO THE
PURPLE

S.L. FLORIAN

ZEBRA BOOKS
KENSINGTON PUBLISHING CORP.

For KSF

ZEBRA BOOKS

are published by

Kensington Publishing Corp.
475 Park Avenue South
New York, NY 10016

First printing: August, 1992

Printed in the United States of America

Prologue

Gather the rose of love, she recited within the canyons of her mind, *whilest yet is time . . .*

The poem, however, went unfinished.

The heavy whirling blackness had been pulling at her for some time now. With a relief that was shot through with something almost akin to pleasure, she let go of her lover's hand and gave in to the greater claim. The last thing she heard as the darkness overcame her was the sound of the siren.

Chapter One

Making Nice

The sudden darkness caused her to sit up.

First she glanced with considerable annoyance at the cloud-covered sun and then began a routine inspection of her long limbs. With a perfectly manicured hand, she began to smooth oil down one leg and then the other, massaging the hard muscles of her calves born of years and years at the barre.

They were good legs, she acknowledged, still lean and sleek after more than twenty-nine years of abuse, though never neglect. Satisfied with the product, she turned over once again and put her headphones back on, noting with a smile of satisfaction the very beginnings of the third Brandenburg Concerto. But still, after several moments of staring at the page, she gave a slight shake of her head and put the bookmark in at page two hundred and sixty-three of Proust's *La Fugitive* and shut the book. Gazing blankly out to sea, she lay thinking.

Delia Giulietta Ross-Merlani knew that her time was running out. As the only child of an aristocratic English Jewess and a wealthy Italian industrialist, she had been educated to the hilt—though precisely to what end had never become quite clear to her. Without much ado, she had attended the best English boarding schools, then Cambridge University, and had even spent a brief interlude at Harvard. And yet after all of this preparation for a life, nearly two years had gone by, and Delia felt herself adrift on a static sea.

She had already discarded all the traditional roles indigenous to her class and consistent with her talents: a brief stint in the Monte Carlo Ballet, a less than idyllic marriage, a short, but unchallenging tenure at Cambridge. Delia knew she had picked up and tossed aside these options with the usual aplomb of the overly talented dilettante. And now, she saw, she had fallen into this haphazard wandering, so reminiscent of her early years, from one tedious watering hole to another.

Delia laid her head back down upon her arms and continued her contemplation of the horizon. Just as the chirping recorders heralded the start of the fourth Brandenburg Concerto, she felt the slight chill of shade once again. Raising her dark head, she beheld the figure of Mr. Gregory MacPhee.

"Miss Delia."

Of all the titles she had held, Professor of Philosophy, Doctor of Letters, Viscountess Ross-Merlani and even briefly, Mrs. Theodore Morgan, the name by which Mr. and Mrs. MacPhee addressed her would always be Delia's favorite. The Scottish couple, now in their late fifties, had been with Delia most of her life—first through her itinerant childhood with her bored, restless mother, and later when she began to live on her own. Between them, Mr. and Mrs. MacPhee filled a number of assorted roles in her life: butler, valet, housekeeper, chauffeur, accountant, social secretary, and majordomo. Using a variety of tactics, most notably a patient cajolery, they had kept and cared for their mistress on several continents, through one marriage and divorce, and in the muddles left behind by numerous lovers of all types.

Although Lady Adela, the Countess of Ross, and Signor Federico Merlani were still very much alive, "Mr. and Mrs. Mac" were the closest things to parents in Delia's canon of emotional fidelities. She had come to understand early on that Adela and Papa were like kindly distant cousins that one sees sporadically; they, were generous with their money and charm, but never with their time or attention.

"Yes, Mr. Mac?"

"This wire just arrived for you."

"Thank you," Delia said as he slit open the envelope and handed it down to her. In spite of his impeccable white linen suit and silk tie, Mr. Mac-Phee looked not at all incongruous among the nude bathers at Nice. Mr. Mac always looked "correct."

Dated the previous night, the telegram read:

Delia,
    Magda in a coma at Lenox Hill Hospital. I
need an ear and shoulder.

Charley

Delia frowned. When was the last time she had
seen Magda Maitland? Could it be a year ago? But
Charley had kept her well informed of Magda's
troubles. Although only two years their senior,
Magda had been in and out of hospitals with a con-
sistency that had astonished her coterie of prominent physicians. Almost monthly, it seemed, Magda
had an ulcer attack, gallstones or some other gruesome gastric complaint. It had not surprised Delia
to learn that Magda had begun to suffer from de-
pressions bordering on melancholia.

Delia hadn't seen her friend Charlotte Maitland
in several months, but neither time nor distance diminished their rapport. They had struck up one
of those instant and life-long friendships that
seem only to happen between very bright and
lonely young girls just as they round into
womanhood. Since their boardings school days,
each woman knew she could count on the other
indefatigably.

Gazing at the telegram again Delia thought,
"Well, an occupation, of a sort, this." Then aloud
she said, "Mr. Mac, we're leaving for New York
straightaway; Magda Maitland is poorly again."
Delia continued her instructions above Mr. Mac-

Phee's murmured *tsk tsk*. "Book us the first available seats to Orly and on to Kennedy. Cable ahead for two suites at the Carlyle, and oh, yes, we'll need a car in New York. Please send a wire to Charlotte: 'Appropriate anatomy appropriated. On my way.' "

"Yes, Miss Delia."

"Have Mrs. Mac leave out my beige Armani suit, St. Laurent red blouse and Amalfi sandals. And do see, *mio cavaliere,* if you can get us a spot of luncheon."

Although no one can click his heels in the sand, Delia Ross-Merlani imagined that somehow she heard this sound as Mr. MacPhee turned abruptly and strode to the hotel to carry out his instructions to the letter.

Delia gazed out of the window as Air France Flight 017 gathered speed out over the Atlantic. She sipped thoughtfully at her glass of cognac and tried once again to gather her scattered thoughts. The tinkling of Mrs. MacPhee's knitting needles was beating out a cadence in counterpoint to Mr. Mac-Phee's gentle snores. She smiled. The simple sounds of their rest comforted her, and for a moment, she put her head back and shut her eyes against the immediacies of the future.

When she opened her eyes again, Delia caught a glimpse of herself reflected in the window; her smile instantly vanished. There was nothing young in the face she studied: no arts left of her youth. A hard face—only softened by the lights from another's bright glance. Charley's smile, she thought, the soft little bow of a mouth that turned so suddenly into a wide, wide beam.

And Magda's. Her exquisite lips, full of promise, could curve into a kitten countenance that delighted. Was that beautiful mouth now twisted in pain as Magda hung between existences? Delia shuddered, trying to shake herself free of the image.

God, she hated illness! Sickness, suffering, death. That *swift* stab of pain in the night. Oh, she had been so frightened! Charley, her new friend, asleep in the next bed, had awakened at her cries and called the house mistress. Delia was nine and had been at boarding school only two weeks.

They had taken her to hospital, and many hands had touched her, hurt her. She remembered vague sensations of burning pain. Then the ether and oblivion.

When she had awakened again, she was in a room that smelled of antiseptic; her stomach hurt horribly. The nurse explained that she was a lucky girl; her appendix had burst just as they had cut her open. "Another hour and you'd have been a goner." The nurse gave her a shot for the pain, and Delia drifted off again.

She awoke and the room was filled with flowers: Adela's and Papa's greetings. "Get well, darling," each had wired from their respective lives. Delia cried then, cried as she had never done, not even when she was sent off to school and Mrs. MacPhee wouldn't stop hugging her goodbye.

12

At a gentle knock on the door, Delia opened her eyes and it seemed as if an angel were gazing down at her. "I'm Magdalene Maitland," the vision explained. "Nurse said Charley's too young to visit, so I came by to cheer you up." And the beautiful mouth broke into that first bright smile. "Delia Giulietta Ross-Merlani! Such a lot of name. What do they call you at home?"

"Delia, sometimes Giulietta. And you?"

"Magda, tho' sometimes Charley says Mags when I'm being bratty."

Delia considered this. She couldn't imagine this lovely girl ever being "bratty." Charlotte's elder sister looked like an icon of the Madonna: violet-blue eyes, white-flaxen hair, palest rose blush.

"I've brought you a present. It's a book of mine, one of my favorites, and I thought you'd like it. It's *so* apropos." She held up a picture book entitled *Madeline*. "It's about a little girl at school, a fearless girl, who has her appendix taken out. Shall I read it to you?" Delia nodded.

Magda sat down on the edge of the bed. Her hair framed her delicate face, and Delia suddenly realized with one of those early prescient moments of last childhood that she was in the company of something outside the ordinary. Magda opened the book then and held up the first picture for Delia to see. In her low, breathy voice, she began to read.

* * *

13

Delia soon fell back to sleep to the beautiful lilting voice. And when she awoke, the book was beside her bed like a talisman to grasp in the night.

Magda had come again and again, bringing books, candies, and messages from Charlotte. She would sit for hours and hours and read aloud. Delia soon learned that Magda had an awesome passion for poetry. The older girl would recite favorite pertinent lines at every turn. This had charmed Delia and been an integral part of their earliest rapport. It was under Magda Maitland's tutelage that Delia's appreciation of poetry was born. And it was this literary love that had laid the foundation of the grown-up Delia's intellectual life.

Yes, over the years, Delia had come to know the "bratty" side of her friend's sister: Magda's ingenuous lies, her disregard for the good opinion of others, her selfishness, her perversity. But through all of this, Delia felt the passionate love Magda had for her younger sister and the tender regard for her sister's friend. "Thank you for loving Charlotte," Magda seemed to say by her countless acts of generosity toward Delia: Magda's scouring the music shops of France and locating a rare score for Delia's dissertation; Magda's flying to Paris to see Delia through her abortion. Magda, never quite her friend, beyond Delia's grasp, but a presence always in her life.

Magda in a coma at Lenox Hill Hospital. Delia now closed her eyes again and tried to

14

picture once more the little book Magda had given her so many years ago. But the image echoing through time and mind could do nothing, Delia knew, to ameliorate the situation, nor to assuage her deepening fears.

Chapter Two

Odds and Ends

"She died about three hours ago," Charlotte Maitland said as she hugged Delia to her.

"Oh, Charley, I'm terribly sorry."

"It's all been so very *peculiar*," Charlotte said rather stiffly.

Delia knew at once from her friend's manner that she was holding back. Understanding this need all too well, Delia gave Charlotte her arm, and the two women sat down together in the living room, side by side.

Charlotte handed Delia a cup of brandy-laced Darjeeling, the traditional hot toddy of their girlhood. Not looking at Delia, Charlotte began to speak as they always did—*in medias res*. "Magda had been feeling so well lately. So very *calm*. She had had such a bad time of it off and on this last year, starting with her operation."

"An investigatory . . . was that what they called it?"

"An exploratory," Charlotte corrected. "They said her appendix seemed fine, but they took it out anyway. Apparently that's standard procedure. But Magda was so dreadfully ill after that."

Delia stared down into her cup and felt a flush rise to her cheeks. Why hadn't she been here for Magda's surgery? she wondered. And then she remembered, and the flush deepened. Papa had summoned her to his villa on the lake for a party he had wished her to host. And then Adela had wanted her to handle that business with the new mare and the hideous Mountjoy's groom, and she hadn't gotten back to New York till a month later. Now it rose in her memory as a time she had failed her friend, and Delia felt she could not forgive herself for it.

"And Jason was such a lamb through it all," Charlotte said, interrupting Delia's unpleasant reverie.

"Had Magda definitely left Ned by then?"

"Oh, yes, once Magda met Jason the marriage with Ned was over. And really, the situation had been intolerable with Ned for so long. For a time after that, things went rather well. Then Magda was rushed off to hospital last Tuesday."

"Her stomach?"

"No, that's the odd thing. She had some kind of fit . . . a seizure, the doctor said. She and Jason were at the movies. Someone called an ambulance. They gave her some medication and she seemed a bit better at first. Then, Jason said, she had another fit. She was comatose by the time they got to hospital. Grand mal seizures, the doctors think. Epilepsy, they say. But there will be a post mortem tomorrow." Charlotte gave a little shudder, and Delia squeezed her friend's cool hands.

"Was Mags still . . . using a great many drugs?"

Charlotte shook her head, and all her soft coppery curls bounced. "No, she stopped everything several months ago. It was a New Year's resolution. Lately, she didn't even *drink* because of her stomach problems. Magda said, 'I don't want to fuck up my body any more than Mother Nature has already.' "

Delia smiled. Yes, that sounded like Magdalene. "Too little, too late?" she asked softly.

"I don't know." Charlotte frowned. "You know what she told me, Delia? She said she no longer needed 'artificial highs.' That being with Jason . . . uh . . . you know . . . making love . . . made her so very happy." In spite of closing in on thirty, Charlotte Frances Maitland still retained a kind of Victorian maidenly innocence when it came to matters sexual. This quality, so totally absent in herself, had always delighted Delia.

Gazing fondly at her friend she asked, "Did you tell the doctors about Magda's drug use?"

Charlotte nodded. "I told the neurologist they called in that Magda had been a steady drug user, or rather abuser, for years. But he said he found no signs of drug involvement."

"What happens now?"

"After the death certificate is signed, we'll have

the funeral. Ned has already rung me up a dozen times wanting to know if I'm 'doing the right thing' for Magda. He's such a pompous ass."

"He's such a *merdeux*," Delia said.

Charlotte nodded in agreement. And then again in that stiff little voice she said, "Thank you for coming, Delia. This whole thing is so dreadful. And with Magda gone . . . you're all I have."

Delia put an arm round Charlotte's slim waist. The two women, their heads together, sat in silence for some time. "Well, you've made good use of the ear, Charley. Need the shoulder?"

Charlotte Maitland looked up at her friend and suddenly let the pent-up tears of the past seventy-two hours fall on Delia's delicate, but sturdy, frame.

"Just you finish that haddie, Miss Delia."

Delia looked up at the sound of Mrs. Mac-Phee's stern dictum. She proceeded to push the now-cold, unappetizing fish around her plate. "What should I wear today, Mrs. Mac? What, do you think, is the appropriate attire to visit a coroner?"

"A what!?"

"A coroner. I'm accompanying Charlotte today to see about the release of Magda's body."

"Oh, it's horrible. This whole business is simply horrible. Poor Miss Maitland."

"Which Miss Maitland do you mean?"

"Why," Mrs. MacPhee said with a reproving

look, "*both* to be sure. But especially poor poor Miss Magdalene. So lovely, she was. I remember that summer the sisters came to Rosemuir. Just before Miss Magda married the professor."

"That *was* a beautiful time," Delia said, pushing away the staring eye of the revolting fish. She suddenly envisioned the three of them bathing in a stream that ran through the Ross lands. They were, she realized, in their innocence almost like some icon of the Three Graces. Yes, that image rang true yet. Magda surely Agalia, that vision of Splendor, delicate yet full-fleshed, every sinew in her seeming to resonate with desire; Charlotte personifying Thalia of Good Cheer, full of warmth and the absolute conviction of one's best; and she herself?—always, always acting the role of Euphrosyne's Mirth, always appearing to laugh at life. How young they had been then—how secure they had seemed in their willingness to embrace all that life might offer. And now, Delia realized, how little prepared the three had been for the lives they had come to lead. "That was the last time Magda truly did look lovely, I do think," she finally said.

"Why don't you like the professor?" Mrs. Mac-Phee asked as she poured another cup of tea for each of them.

"No human being of quality can like Edward Hennessey," Delia pronounced. "He's like someone out of a Brontë novel gone bad: Heathcliff without his sex appeal, Mr. Rochester without his brusque charm."

Mrs. MacPhee clucked. "Well, he must have

something the folks here like. A man doesn't get to be head of a university department without possessing something good."

Delia got up and kissed the top of Mrs. Mac-Phee's tightly anchored braids. "Ah, you are such an innocent. If I had a penny for every out and out *trou du cul* that became a successful academic, we should be showered in copper. No, all that Ned Hennessey possesses is a great deal of information about English history and a beautiful red beard. He once had the love of Magdalene Maitland, something quite special I should think, but he crushed it. And her, too." Cup in hand, Delia began to wander restlessly about the suite.

Mrs. MacPhee observed her mistress for a moment and then asked, "Why do you think Miss Magda married him?"

Delia paused in the act of sipping her tea. "I don't know, actually. I always meant to ask Charlotte about that," she said. "But Mags was always doing odd things." Delia made a mental note to ask her friend if she knew why Magdalene *had* married Ned. Odd as Magda could be, Ned had certainly been so outside the circle of her usual cohorts.

"You'd never have thought to see Miss Magda that she was sickly. She looked as pure as an angel, she did," Mrs. MacPhee said. "Whatever was ailing that child?"

Delia began to twirl a strand of hair round her fingers, saw Mrs. MacPhee's disapproving glance, and stopped. "Oh, it was a kind of a snowball effect this last year. Magda had all those stomach problems for a time and was finally operated on. The doctors didn't find much, but I gather from Charley that Mags was quite ill for a while after the surgery."

"Doctors!" Mrs. MacPhee grumbled disparagingly. "And then wasn't there some business with her teeth?"

"Yes, poor Mags, nothing seemed to go right for her." Delia gave a thoughtful tap with her long nail to her own slightly imperfect set of enamels: there was a tiny gap between her two front teeth. "Her wisdom teeth gave her no end of bother. The top ones were taken out by the dentist, I remember, but then the bottom two became impacted." Delia gave a shiver. "Had to be *surg*ically removed. And then, as if that weren't enough, Magda had a terrible stomach attack just a few days after that. No wonder she was depressed. I remember a note she sent me in Paris last year telling me to direct all her mail to Lenox Hill Hospital as she had decided simply to move in. *Pauvre, pauvre,* Magdalene."

"Well, at least now, she's been put to rest."

"Yes," Delia said softly, imagining the shimmering image of Magdalene Maitland, "to rest." After another silence, Delia blithely inquired, "So what's the verdict?"

"On what?"

"Proper attire."

"Your navy Pauline Trigère."

"The one with the jacket? *Minchione!* Mrs.

22

Mac, that looks like widows' weeds. No, I want to wear something to ward off the chill of the morgue—something beautiful, fantastical."

As Delia got into the Mercedes limousine, she smoothed down the skirt of her Oscar de la Renta dress. She loved the iridescent mauve pattern which seemed to set off the richness of her tawny tan. Looking into the mirror Mr. MacPhee had stationed in the backseat, she adjusted her hat. Delia *always* wore a hat, perhaps her acknowledged vestige of having an English mother. From beneath the large brim, her two sloe eyes beamed. At school, Delia had once had a lover from Athens who said her eyes were the color of the green depths of the Aegean. She had tired of him rather quickly, but let him make love to her again and again because he would kiss and court her eyes. Taking a lip brush from her purse, she applied a bit more gloss to her generous mouth. The full bottom lip, she'd always believed, was an "endearing" flaw. Today, for once, the face gazing back at Delia seemed wholly satisfying to the beholder.

When Charlotte Maitland got into the car, the two friends hugged each other tightly. They seemed to linger close to one another as if their proximity would provide solace and strength. Ten minutes later, the Mercedes pulled up in front of the Chief Medical Examiner's Office on First Avenue. They were ushered into a small office to await the assistant medical examiner assigned to the Hennessey case.

In the few minutes they waited in tense silence, Delia studied the effects of the room. In spite of the simple bureaucratic furniture and bland walls, the resident had managed to make the room look singular. There were several tremendous asparagus ferns, their feathers catching the morning light. The walls were lined with books, many of them legal and medical texts, but, Delia noted with some surprise, several shelves contained volumes of English and Irish poetry. Her eye was then caught by the exquisite desk set, the pieces heavy blond Italian marble. She was mildly surprised not to find any gilt-framed photos; the desk set seemed the perfect gift from a woman to her lover.

Suddenly, the door opened. "Good morning, Ms. Maitland, I'm Dr. Elliot."

Both women turned to look at the official, and Charlotte automatically extended a hand. "Good morning, Doctor. This is my friend, Dr. Ross-Merlani."

"What specialty?" Dr. Elliot asked as he shook Delia's hand.

"Medieval Studies," Delia said, pronouncing the syllables in staccato. "And it's *Ms*. Ross-Merlani. My ever-hopeful friend still uses my academic title in spite of the fact that I haven't set foot in a university quad two years Trinity term."

"I see," the doctor replied, obviously a bit bewildered by this onrush of information. "Well, I'm

24

glad to make your acquaintance. I'm terribly sorry about the circumstances." Charlotte murmured her thanks and then began to discuss the sordid but necessary details with Dr. Elliot.

Delia, as was often her wont, tuned the conversation out as one would the static interfering with a symphony. She had always prided herself on her powers of observation, and now she sat quietly for some time. From beneath her hat, Delia studied the rather intriguing figure of Dr. Daniel Elliot.

He was tall, at least six feet, and quite slim. But Delia's practiced eye conjured up well-developed arms and a smooth chest. Behind a pair of horn-rimmed spectacles were two of the darkest, deepest eyes she had ever seen. Not even in Italy or the south of Spain had she encountered such eyes like polished onyx. His hair, thick, almost thatchy-looking, was the red-brown of the horn rims. There was a kind of pinkish cast to his complexion which many redheads had; Delia wondered if he had been a freckle-faced lad. Daniel Elliot was looking grave now as he spoke, but she easily imagined the small lines round his lips and eyes when he smiled. Suddenly Delia was called back to her place and time as she noticed Charlotte's trembling mouth.

"Apparently, then," Dr. Elliot was intoning, "your sister had no previous history of neurological disturbances? Dizziness? Light-headedness?"

Charlotte colored and said softly, "Well, she had had . . . some blackouts."

"Blackouts?" Dr. Elliot asked. "What kind of blackouts?"

Charlotte frowned. "I don't rightly know. All Magda told me was that she'd had some periods of blacking out this last year. She would . . . it seems . . . well . . . lose consciousness. When she awoke, she could never quite recall fainting, though."

"Didn't she report this to her physician?"

Charlotte shook her head. "No."

"Why not?" Dr. Elliot asked rather abruptly. Then seeing Charlotte's startled response, the doctor recovered his composure and said, "Why wouldn't your sister discuss this with her doctor? Surely in this day and age, epilepsy is not something to be ashamed of. . . ."

"I imagine," Charlotte replied in a small but steady voice, "that my sister hadn't the vaguest notion of epilepsy and believed her blackouts were caused by the drugs she used. Therefore this would not be something she discussed with her physicians. However, the blackouts must have frightened her a good deal because Magda stopped taking drugs altogether."

"Well, not quite altogether," Daniel Elliot said smoothly. "We found small traces of secobarbital sodium in Mrs. Hennessey's bloodstream. But not even close to toxic or for that matter even effective levels."

"Seconal?" Delia asked. The doctor nodded. Delia raised one eyebrow. She had always had a particular dislike of unclear edges and loose ends and suddenly this one began to unravel in her mind. "How very odd," she thought, "Magda had told Charley that she had stopped using drugs. Why would she lie about a few sedatives when she had always confided all those rococo details of her drug use?"

Delia's thoughts were interrupted by Charlotte's voice. "Did my sister's gastritis play any part in her death?"

Dr. Elliot ran a hand across his chin. "No, and I'm not so sure your sister had any gastric problems. We found no evidence of either gallstones or ulcers upon autopsy."

"But my sister was hospitalized *many* times for her stomach attacks. How can that be?"

Charlotte began now to chew her lower lip in a gesture Delia knew so well. Rushing in to her friend's aid she said, "Doctor, Magda suffered from severe bouts of depression and was seeing an analyst. Might those attacks have been psychosomatic? A symptom of some kind of emotional illness?"

Dr. Elliot studied Delia Ross-Merlani for a moment. Her voice, with its peremptory tone, set him on edge. He disliked her type: old money looking down its aristocratic nose. He realized how much he resented being put on the defensive by her. Coldly he replied, "Perhaps, but diseases of the mind are not *my* specialty. Mrs. Hennessey died in a coma of respiratory failure brought on by *Status epilepticus*."

Delia frowned. "Jargon," she thought. Medical

jargon, which she knew was meant to put her at a disadvantage by pointing up the doctor's credentials and her lack thereof. Supercilious bastard! she concluded with not some little satisfaction.

"All the papers are ready, Ms. Maitland. You can have the funeral director contact this number to make the arrangements." He stood up, indicating the interview was over. Shaking hands once again with both women, appropriate murmurs of thanks and condolence were exchanged.

Back in the car, Delia studied Charlotte's face. There was none of the unhappiness or pain or even relief she had expected to find. Instead, she read bewilderment there. Charley's moue just then reminded Delia of the way her friend had looked as she had tried in vain more than a dozen years ago to put together the pieces of a geometry proof. So, Charlotte had felt those loose ends, too, Delia thought.

Throughout the next days, that puzzled expression remained just at the edges of Charlotte Maitland's eyes. And it was soon refracted and reflected in Delia's own increasingly troubled gaze.

Chapter Three

Funeral Games

At the back of the chapel stood Lady Delia Ross-Merlani, her eyes fixed upon the Star of David and filled with some bewilderment. This was not the first time in her life that she knew she felt distinctly out of place. Although half-Jewish by birth, Delia's religious sense was nearly nonexistent. If she believed in anything, she'd always told her Cambridge friends when the subject arose as it often did over coffee and stale tobacco smoke late at night, it was *Spiritus Mundi*. Lady Adela Ross had had, of course, little interest in the religion of her ancestors and had passed on a kind of foreboding to her daughter about all things Judaic. Being in Debrett rather than being devout was *de rigueur* in the Ross family.

Signor Merlani was as indifferent to his Catholicism as he was to his wife and daughter. Delia knew that whatever swam into her father's field of vision could capture the industrialist's attention for a short while. Without much thought on either of their parts, Delia had attended Midnight Mass with her father when she had taken her school holidays in Italy. Signor Merlani had on these occasions often fallen asleep while his daughter wove tales about the pageants before her.

Like Magda and Charlotte Maitland, Delia was a Jew in name only. With the two sisters, she had attended chapel at boarding school each day. The three had treated this required observance with the same equanimity as they had all the rites of passage in a traditional English education.

Today however, her ladyship was troubled by the conundrum of belonging to, yet feeling estranged from, the service being conducted before her. The language, the gestures, the very tenor of the place felt so alien to her. Jews connoted only strange clothing, loud voices and the disenfranchised. Where in her history had she lost her connection to this past? she wondered. Shaking off these confused thoughts, Delia was about to advance to her seat beside Charlotte when the upright figure of Professor Edward Hennessey caught her eye.

Delia's response to Ned was, as always, immediate and visceral: she recoiled. Something about him seemed to belie his vaguely handsome, scholarly mien. Without any definite reason, she had always found Magda's husband to be somewhat sinister. But just as some people cannot tear their gaze from a gruesome accident, Delia felt unable to dismiss Ned Hennessey from her mind and sight.

With an effort, she slowly turned her look of inquiry on the little silver-haired woman next to Ned. Ah, yes, Delia thought, the matriarch, Mother Hennessey. This face was set in a grim, hard line, and Delia saw in it the same unrelenting lights she had seen in the son's face. Next to Mrs. Hennessey, carefully kept in tow, was Patrick, her younger son. Having failed to keep Ned in line ("His marriage to me," Delia recalled Magda reporting once to her, "is viewed as a catastrophe second only to the Great Potato Famine."), Mrs. Hennessey took no chances with her last child. From Magda's and Charlotte's descriptions, Delia knew that Patrick was kept constantly at his mother's beck and call, relied on, bullied, babied.

Hadn't there been something unpleasant about Patrick . . . something Charley had mentioned a while back? Oh, yes, he had told Magda that he was "violently in love" with her . . . yes . . . now Delia remembered. Mrs. Hennessey and Patrick had come to stay with Ned and Magda in their country place at Whitinsville . . . in Western Massachusetts . . . when was it? . . . she'd have to ask Charley when—and there had been a nasty scene. A declaration was it, a fumbling, a fight? Looking at the Hennessey clan, Delia gave a slight shudder. *Merde!* What an unappetizing lot, she thought.

After a long moment, she was, however, jolted back to reality by the sound of Charlotte's soft sobs. Delia hurried to her friend's side. The ceremony, short, impressive yet still distinctly remote, finally ended, and everyone filed out to waiting limousines for the trip to the cemetery. Delia was steering the now-silent, but rigid Charlotte into the Mercedes when a young man rushed up to her friend and threw his arms about Charlotte's neck, sobbing.

This brought fresh tears to Charlotte's eyes. "Oh, Jason," she murmured again and again.

During this little drama, Delia took the opportunity to study Jason Howland. He was decidedly handsome, she thought, and surprisingly young—perhaps twenty-two or -three. Although tall and broad, Magda's last lover had that terribly endearing look of a lost puppy, and Delia determined at once to like him.

Mrs. MacPhee managed to soothe the sorrowing pair, and introductions were exchanged. At last, Charlotte, Mrs. MacPhee and Jason got into the limousine. As she checked to see that all was settled, Delia felt a tap on her shoulder. She turned to face Edward Hennessey.

"I believe I should accompany Charlotte."

His icy tone made Delia's eyes narrow. "I can't think why."

"Because," he said, his voice low, "I *am* Magda's husband."

Delia suddenly had the deepest regret for taking that rash vow of nonviolence in her trendy post-sixties girlhood: she wanted very much to smash Ned Hennessey's smug face. "You *were* Magda's husband. That became past tense long before her death. I do not intend to let you upset Charley."

"I have no intention of upsetting Charlotte. Merely of taking my rightful place by her side."

This idea of "right" was the very thing that had always most irritated Delia about him. There was no sincerity in this man, she knew, only propriety.

A sudden commotion could be heard from inside the car. Jason emerged finally, his face a mask from Greek tragedy. "Your rightful place, you bastard! Your rightful place is in that box instead of my beautiful Magdalene. You bastard, you hateful bastard, you murderer." With all the agility of a young cat, Jason leapt upon the other man, knocking him to the ground.

"You killed her with your hate! You killed her," Jason screamed as he pummelled Ned's soft body. Magda's husband put up no resistance in spite of being Jason's equal in size if not youthful vigor.

At a nod from Delia, Mr. MacPhee—who'd been a boxer as a lad and still golfed eighteen three times a week—coolly pulled the kicking

33

and now-hysterical Jason off Ned and bundled the sobbing man back into the car. Quickly, Delia hopped in and slammed the door shut after her. As the car pulled away, she glimpsed once again the figure of Ned Hennessey, now flanked by his family. He was nonchalantly straightening his tie as if violence were his everyday deserts.

"Whatever is wrong, Miss Delia?" Mrs. MacPhee inquired in a whisper. "You gave such a start!"

Delia shook her head as her eyes gazed off into the distance. The look of mundane malevolence on Edward Hennessey's face had left her all cold with horror. And then, almost with a jolt, she imagined she heard Magda's voice, suddenly so clear in the air around her: *Cruelty has a human heart,/ And Jealousy a human face;/ Terror the human form divine,/ And Secrecy the human dress*. Delia gave another shudder. "Just a sudden chill," she said, taking Mrs. MacPhee's hand into her own.

Chapter Four

The Mouths of Babes

"Charley?"

"Hmmm?"

"Listen, I want to ask you a question." Delia raised herself on an elbow and faced Charlotte's form. The two women had spent the morning playing squash at the Harvard Club. Now lying on their stomachs, wrapped in sheets, they were resting after being expertly pounded by the club's masseuse.

"Yes?"

"Why do you think Mags married Ned?"

Charlotte looked up. Her face was moist and flushed, wet curls clinging to her scalp. She seemed very young in spite of her look of stern consternation. "Why indeed! I guess she was attracted to him, his solidness, his certainty."

"Was she in love with him, do you think?"

"At first? Oh, I imagine so. He was so different from her usual men. All her 'friends' were so

. . . lightweight. Ned seemed so self-assured. Magda told me once that Ned was the first person who took *her* seriously."

"A very attractive trait, that," Delia murmured.

"In some ways Ned seemed to imbue everything with a reality — something that Magda obviously needed, and kept coming back to." Charlotte paused. "No matter how dreadful things became, he seemed to take them in stride and would somehow straighten them out. Or so I think Magda always believed. He was a kind of father figure, I imagine."

"*Less* attractive, that," Delia said, not without some irritation in her voice. "Depends on the father, I should think."

Charlotte looked at her friend but let this painful reference pass. She knew better than to engage Delia in any discussion about her parents.

A charged silence followed; finally Charlotte said, "Delia, do you remember the film *Rashomon* — we saw it in Paris, with Magda. . . ."

"Yes, of course."

"I was just thinking about it . . . about the film. Do you believe there are different versions of truth — or one actual truth?"

Delia frowned. "I don't quite know. Flaubert says something about there being nothing really true — only that we each have our own ways of seeing the truth. Why do you ask, Charley?"

"I see my sister one way, Dr. Elliot another, Ned another, and Jason his own way. Who is to say what she truly was?" Delia watched then in some surprise as her friend bolted upright and large tears began to roll down her face. "I can say! *I knew her! I know her!*"

Getting up off the table, Charlotte began to pace the small room, wiping the tears from her chin and cheeks with the back of her hand. And at that moment, Delia realized that she had gotten that image all wrong of the Three Graces. No, she now saw that she and these two sisters had lived more the myth of those three goddesses whom Paris had had to judge. Magda had indeed been Venus, that apotheosis of Love that a man would do anything for, anything to possess; and she now saw herself as Hera, that constantly striving and imperious goddess queen, trying always to shape the world to her own unclear ends. And suddenly here was Charlotte taking on the accoutrements of that goddess of Homer's description: Athena, ready to do battle for what is true. And Delia's heart opened once again and embraced her friend, grateful to have this woman with her generous spirit and staunch integrity be such a constant in her own sometimes slippery life.

When Charlotte spoke, her voice was firm now. "Magda said she had stopped taking drugs. She told me that of her own accord. She knew how I felt, how I had always felt, about that as-

37

pect of her life. Even the unhappiness it gave me hadn't motivated her to stop or to change. But when her illnesses came one after another and the blackouts began, she decided to stop on her own. She told me so!" Charlotte paused, and her eyes looked out beyond the room, framing this memory. "I watched her on New Year's Day as she emptied her . . . stash—that's what she called it—down the toilet. Red pills, yellow pills, hashish, Valium, something called 'Ludes' . . . and cocaine. It was like a little ceremony, a burial! She flushed it all away. And she hugged me and then we laughed. We celebrated by going out for gelato . . . and Mags insisted they put some of those sprinkles on hers . . ." Charlotte's voice caught in her throat, but after a moment she recovered again and said, "She was *very* happy."

Delia listened and considered her friend's words. Certainly the image of Magdalene Maitland flushing away a fortune in drugs was provocative, and she didn't for a moment discount the authenticity of Charlotte's account, but. . . .

"Delia?"

"Yes."

"Magda *did not* take the drugs Dr. Elliot found in her body. Someone must have given them to her . . . given them to her perhaps without her knowing."

Delia's eyes met her friend's, and very gently

38

she said, "Even so, Charley. As Dr. Elliot said, that didn't kill her."

"We don't *know* that! Oh, maybe there were other drugs that made her ill—weakened her. We don't know what happened. *But I must know, Delia.* Don't you see? I must know if the sister I buried yesterday was indeed the one I knew and loved. I must know. Please, Delia, please."

Charlotte's eyes were huge now as she looked at her friend in appeal. Delia recognized this at once. She had seen it countless times during their years together: Charlotte's plea that Delia, the stronger, the more courageous, the more clever, look out for the pitfalls for her friend. Delia looked again at Charlotte and suddenly saw in her tear-stained countenance the vision of that other friend: the searching sweet-sad eyes of Magdalene. "Yes, Charley. I'll find out."

Both women lay back down once more; one to rest in the protective gaze of her friend, the other with the knowledge that she must wander once again through those fun-house mirror images of what is true.

Chapter Five

Gentlemen Callers

Delia pushed the breakfast things away from her and stretched into a great yawn. "I shan't need either of you darlings today," she said, addressing Mrs. MacPhee. "Take the afternoon off."

"And where should we be off to?" Mrs. MacPhee asked tartly. She knew they were being dismissed for the afternoon and immediately wondered about her mistress's motives.

Delia smiled brightly. "Why not take in a matinée?"

"You won't be needing the car, then, Miss Delia?" queried Mr. MacPhee.

"No, I shall be entertaining here. I'm having guests for luncheon and tea."

"Who are your guests?" Mrs. MacPhee asked, readying to prepare the correct costume for her ladyship.

"Jason Howland for luncheon, Professor Hennessey for tea."

Mrs. MacPhee's eyebrow shot up in exact duplication of Delia's look of surprise. They had long since lost the knowledge of the gesture's origin. "Professor Hennessey having tea with you?"

"Yes, as a hostess, I'm in *such* demand."

"Whatever do you want to see him for?" Mrs. MacPhee asked, ignoring Delia's last remark.

"Oh, there's heaps of stuff I'll be helping Charley handle . . . getting Magda's things . . . settling the estate. I thought it best to mend fences with Professor Neddie."

"And Mr. Howland?"

Delia smiled. "He seems such a sweet lamb, doesn't he? He's very fond of Charlotte, and I have the feeling she's going to need the love and support of everyone around her. Magda's death is such a blow."

"For Miss Charlotte?" Mr. MacPhee inquired, looking intently over his copy of *The Times* at his mistress.

"For everyone," Delia said softly, looking up to meet the sympathetic gaze she knew she would find.

Delia Ross-Merlani welcomed Jason Howland to a lavish luncheon with just the right mixture of warmth and formality. She was dressed in a pair of Bill Blass linen pants and the silk blouse

41

her maternal grandmother had been given by Coco Chanel when they'd been young together in Paris. Jason, she thought, looked far more attractive in his jeans and sweater than in the stylish suit she had last seen him in.

He came forward and gave her a gentle kiss on the cheek. "Thank you for . . . uh . . . taking care of things the other day . . . at the . . . uh . . . service. Magda spoke of you often—she knew you were a special friend."

"Will you talk a bit about her, Jason? About your relationship. I'd like to know. Sort of tie it all up, you see."

"Oh, yes," he said eagerly. "To put her to rest, I . . . uh . . . understand." His voice caught a bit in his throat. "Rest . . . that's what my poor Magda was really looking for."

"How did the two of you meet?"

He laughed. "At the dentist. Can you believe it? Magda had just had a wisdom tooth pulled and was sitting in the waiting room till she felt less dizzy. God, she was beautiful! Her golden hair was all sort of frizzy and like a halo. I must have been staring at her because she gave me a crooked smile . . . you know . . . because of the Novocain. Then she laughed . . . felt silly, I guess.

"When I came out after my appointment, she was just getting ready to leave." He grinned. "She told me later she'd waited for me. Anyway, we rode down in the elevator together, joking

. . . you know . . . dentist jokes. Neither of us could eat for an hour, so we sat in a booth in a bar and drank ale. When Magda's Novocain wore off, we switched to vodka. We got drunk—but nice drunk . . . you know—and came back to my place and made love. And we were together from then on."

"What about Ned?"

Jason's face flushed with anger. "At first, Magda and I met secretly. Then she confronted Ned and moved in with me."

"As simply as that?" Delia's voice betrayed none of the incredulity she felt. She couldn't imagine Ned simply stepping aside nor down.

"Yeah. Magda said it was Ned's latest stance—'The Martyred Husband.' But we were so happy—we didn't care. Everything was beautiful . . . until . . . the stomach pains began."

"When did that happen?"

"Well, she'd had them off and on before she met me, you know. About three months after we began to live together things got pretty bad. Her stomach really bothered her a lot. She stopped drinking and watched her diet."

"No liquor at all?"

"Uh-uh, the doctors said she was having bouts of acute gastritis and should be real careful. For a while, Magda was even into health foods." He grimaced then as he chewed with gusto on the *Sole Coquelin* provided.

"What about drugs?" Delia carefully studied

Jason's face. He looked young, very young, she realized, and that made her feel rather old suddenly. But she turned her attention back to him.

"No drugs. Her shrink wanted to prescribe a sedative, but Magda refused. 'No dope,' she said. And she was kind of proud of that."

"Sounds very commendable," Delia said, unable to reconcile the "New Magda" with the image of the high-lifer she knew her late friend had been.

"We began to talk about a future together. I've never been any great shakes as an actor, and Magda was getting fed up with the New York art scene. We thought we might move some place quiet . . . you know . . . open an antique shop. Settle down, marry, have kids." His voice had become dreamy.

"Marry?"

"Oh, yes. Magda had told Ned she wanted a divorce so she could marry me." His voice cracked. "It was going to be such a beautiful life, with my beautiful Magdalene." Jason began to weep softly, and Delia made soothing sounds as she handed him a snifter of brandy.

After her first guest's departure, Delia sat down for a few moments to collect her thoughts. Could it be? Could Love indeed have worked a miracle in Magdalene Maitland Hennessey? Could she really have planned such an idyllic fu-

44

ture with this sweet, sweet boy?

A loud rap on the door brought Delia back to her senses. There was an awkward silence as Edward Hennessey came in. "I've ordered tea. Will Earl Grey do?" Delia asked as they shook hands.

"Lipton's would have been fine. I'm no connoisseur."

She motioned him to a chair. "I'm frightfully sorry, Ned, about the other day. Everyone had a dreadful case of nerves. We all behaved rather badly, I fear."

Ned shrugged, and Delia thought he looked like a bloated bull. This apology had not come easily to her lips, and Delia was most annoyed at his graceless acceptance of it.

"Charlotte is still quite distressed, as you might imagine. She's asked me to kind of sort things out for her."

"Like what?"

"I'd like to collect Magda's clothes and such. Is there much at your place?"

"All of my wife's belongings except for a few items are in *our* home. I'll go through them and crate what Charlotte may have."

Delia suppressed a shudder of disgust. "I'm surprised that Magda left so much with you. I understood she'd been living with Jason Howland these last months."

"Magda picked up and discarded lifestyles as some women try new hairdos. Jason Howland was just another passing fancy—'Young Lover Chic,' I should call it."

Both lapsed into silence when the waiter came in and served tea. Then with cup poised in hand, Delia said carefully, "I thought Magda had asked for a divorce."

Ned Hennessey stirred his tea for several seconds. "That's ridiculous. I would never have divorced Magda. Nor would she ever have divorced me. *Never.*"

"Are you so sure?" Delia asked, not bothering now to disguise the hostility in her voice.

"Listen, Delia, I lived with Magdalene for nearly eleven years. I knew all her little secrets. All her little tricks. She couldn't make a life without me—and she knew that." His voice had become hard, ugly. He stood up abruptly. "Tell Charlotte I'll have my wife's things sent to her. Goodbye, Delia."

She stood up, too, and watched him go. He was a tall, gaunt kind of a man; she liked nothing about him, she knew. He seemed to find pleasure in small triumphs, and she was a woman who strived always for greater glories.

When left alone, Delia suddenly felt unclean, tainted. She quickly stripped and jumped into a steaming tub into which she poured generous amounts of scent and oil. Then, wrapped in one of the plum-colored velvet robes Mrs. Mac had been making for her since girlhood, Delia sat upon the bed, her knees drawn up under her.

Something, she knew, was wrong. The pieces didn't fit. Jason *and* Ned couldn't be right. Yet each had seemed so sure of himself and Magda.

"Another snag," she thought. *"Quel emmerdement!* It's time, I should think, for me to pull some strings of my own."

Delia got out a thick leatherbound volume from the desk. She leafed through the many listings and copious interlinear notes for some time. Finally, she found what she wanted and, with the Cheshire Cat's smile, picked up the phone and dialed.

Chapter Six

Knit One, Purl Two

Daniel Elliot stared at the phone, willing it not to ring. He felt particularly disinclined this morning to talk to Sheila. Closing his eyes, he tried to visualize the body and face of the woman he had been to bed with the night before. But couldn't. Sheila melted into Sharon, Sharon into Sheryl and so on, stretching backward through the succession of meaningless affairs that had filled these last months.

He stood for a moment looking down at the morass of paperwork on his desk. Unwilling to begin his work, he occupied several moments watering his plants. Then he lazily slit open some obviously unimportant mail, attempting further distraction. Just as he felt himself backed up against the wall of duty, a knock came as a welcome interruption. His chief stuck his head in the door.

"Got a minute, Dan?"

"Sure, take a seat."

Daniel watched as George Felton perched himself on the edge of a chair. "What's up?" Daniel said.

"Remember the Hennessey case—a couple of weeks back?"

"Yes, vaguely. Why?"

"Well, it seems that the family is . . . well, unsatisfied with the final report."

Daniel visualized the image of Charlotte Maitland and then suddenly pictured her friend. His face contracted into an amused frown. "You must be kidding. It was a piece of cake."

"Well, yes," George said, "but there seem to be some inquiries now that we have to . . . uh . . . follow up on."

"Inquiries?"

"Yes," George said, and he looked distinctly uncomfortable. "A Ms. Ross-Merlani has several questions she wants answered, and our office has been asked to cooperate."

"Asked?" Daniel said dryly.

"Uh . . . yes."

"By whom?"

"Let's just say by the powers that be."

"Shit!" Daniel replied. "I'm up to my ass in work, George. I don't have time to screw around with crap like this."

"I'm afraid you have to. We're to 'assist Ms. Ross-Merlani in every way.' "

Daniel nodded, seeing it was hopeless to protest. "Okay. Let her make an appointment — I'll try to squeeze her in."

George gave an embarrassed smile. "Her car is picking you up at noon." Daniel opened his mouth to object, and George quickly added, "At least you'll get a lunch out of it."

When he was alone, Daniel again studied the mass of papers still before him. He was now filled with an intense desire to get to work. "Fuck Ms. Ross-Merlani," he murmured.

Then he sat down, put his feet up and focused on the image of his lunch date. Although put out, he was not, he realized with surprise, entirely displeased at the prospect of the coming encounter.

The maître d' at Olympe snapped to attention at the sight of the young woman in the broad-brimmed hat. "Good afternoon, Lady Delia. How lovely to see you again."

"Thank you, Gerard. Dr. Elliot and I would like to sample some of your superb fare."

Gerard seemed to grow taller under the obvious flattery as he led them to a table laden with flowers and crystal. In a moment, unbidden, he brought a bottle of Perrier-Jouët champagne and two fluted glasses. As he poured the wine, he listed the specific delicacies that might interest her ladyship. Without consulting her companion, Delia dictated the order to the smiling maître d'.

Daniel Elliot waited until they were alone and then spoke up in his soft, firm voice. "*Lady* Delia?"

Delia made a wry face. "Yes. It's yet another title I don't much fancy . . . Lady Delia Ross-Merlani . . . the Ross is from my mother's side, the Ross family of Surrey. But it comes in handy for restaurants and queues."

Daniel noted this Anglicism and asked, "Then, you are a born and bred Englishwoman?"

Delia shook her head. "No, my father is Italian, but most of my education was English."

"Ross-Merlani," her companion said, rolling the words round his tongue, "sounds like an apéritif."

Delia's eyes turned steely. "Not very original, that. Nearly everyone says it upon meeting me."

The color rose in Daniel Elliot's face. Something about those green-blue eyes staring at him from beneath the picturesque hat vaguely unnerved him. "Sorry," he said at last, "I don't usually run to type. I'll try a little harder in the future."

There was an uncomfortable silence between them for several moments as they picked at the scallop, endive and escarole salad in front of them. Then Daniel said, "Well, *Ms.* Ross-Merlani, this lunch was your idea. What can I do for you?"

Delia sipped at the champagne and then said in measured tones, "I'm unsatisfied with some of

51

the details surrounding Magda Maitland's death."

"You mean Magda Hennessey?"

Delia grimaced in an almost childlike way. "Yes, I suppose that's so." He waited and she went on. "Something doesn't quite jell, quite make sense."

"Such as?"

Delia let out a breath. "You see, Magda was always . . . well, reckless—even when we were girls. Although Charlotte is two years younger than Magda, she always rather mothered her elder sister. Their parents were killed when the girls were quite young, so they were always very close.

"But Magda never hid anything from Charlotte. It was even a kind of joke between them— Mags called Charley her 'Mother Confessor.' She confided even her worst peccadillos to Charley. No matter how duplicitous her life became with others, Magda *never* lied to her sister."

"Why duplicitous?" Dr. Elliot interrupted.

Delia smiled. "Being adventurous was almost a religion with Magda. 'Do anything, do everything,' she used to say, 'no matter what the cost.' Magda saw herself," Delia said musingly, "as a combination of Camille, Lady Macbeth, and the Lady From Shanghai. But some part of her had to touch base now and then. So Magda went to school, got married and had an intermittently successful career as an art historian." Delia paused and then said thoughtfully, "Hiding her penchant for the demimonde added a certain fillip to it—or so Magda always maintained."

As she spoke, Delia was studying Daniel Elliot's face. She noticed the flicker of interest evoked by the exotica that had been Magdalene Maitland Hennessey. He seemed almost aroused by her description, she realized.

The doctor's face lapsed once more into impassivity as he became aware of his companion's scrutiny. "Go on," he said, his tone neither encouraging nor discouraging.

"Several months ago, Magda told Charlotte, in fact *insisted,* that she had stopped taking all drugs. Her blackouts apparently frightened her into some prudence. Yet you found Seconal in her body."

Daniel nodded. "But the level was insignificant and couldn't have been the precipitating factor in her death."

Delia paused as the waiter set their entrées down in front of them. Then with a practiced precision, she extracted a piece of lobster from its tail, dipped it into the lightly scented butter and popped it delicately into her mouth. Looking up, she saw Dr. Elliot's eyes riveted upon her. Uncharacteristically, Delia flushed.

With a conscious effort, she recovered her composure and said, "The *level* may be insignificant, but the fact of the drug being there at all *is* significant. Magda told Charlotte that she was not using any drugs. *Ergo,* Magda either lied or did not take the drugs of her own volition. Either way, I intend to know the answer."

The medical examiner looked at her for a moment. "To tell you the truth, *Lady* Delia Ross-Merlani," he said, "I don't give a fuck about your friend and her drug-toting habits. Dozens of senseless deaths take place in this city every day, and I barely have time to cope with those. However"—and here his voice hardened—"you obviously think it might make an amusing anecdote to share with your friends on the Côte d'Azur. Fine. You chase down your answers. But don't ask me to expend my valuable time playing your games." He rose from his seat.

Delia drew back then. She saw for a brief moment how Dr. Daniel Elliot must see her: self-important, insignificant, ridiculous. Something in her needed and sought always the good opinion of others; Delia suddenly felt overcome with an intense vulnerability. Without thought, she reached out a hand and touched his wrist. "Please," she said, "I'm sorry. I really do not intend to take up your time with trifles. Give me a moment to make you understand." The doctor's face remained fixed.

Delia groped for the right words to explain the ambiguous sense she felt pulling at her. Something vague, something on the edge of her perception focused as she recalled the books lining Dr. Elliot's walls. Then in the next instant she pictured Magda's beautiful face: haunting, perverse, triumphant with false promises and broken dreams. She heard again Magda's voice reciting favorite lines. Delia's eyes met Daniel Elliot's and very slowly she echoed her friend's words:

> " 'Are they shadows that we see?
> And can shadows pleasure give?
> Pleasures only shadows be,
> Cast by bodies we conceive,
> And are made the things we deem
> In those figures which they seem.' "

"Marlowe?" Daniel Elliot asked.

"No, a somewhat more obscure contemporary of his—Samuel Daniel. He wrote a cycle of 'Delia' sonnets." Her companion nodded, and Delia realized she had to give him some credit: it wasn't every man who could correctly spot a quote from the Elizabethans. She saw, however, that she had gotten his attention once again. "You see," she explained carefully, "for Charlotte and me there is an inconsistency in how we ultimately see Magda Maitland. We don't know how she . . . turned out. And that's very important to us. I'd simply like to finish the picture of my friend."

Daniel Elliot considered this for a moment and then said, "I have very sensitive antennae for these things, Ms. Ross-Merlani, but in Mrs.

Hennessey's case I didn't perceive even the vaguest signal of anything wrong."

Delia smiled to herself. She liked his image of antennae and tried to decide exactly where upon his most attractive person Daniel Elliot's receivers were located.

"However," he said, meeting her eyes, "I admire your sense of loyalty. Ms. Maitland is fortunate in having such a steadfast friend."

"I see, Doctor," Delia said slowly, "that you *are* true to your word." He looked puzzled and she was pleased. "You certainly aren't running *quite* to type."

Delia found herself rewarded with a becoming flush spreading across her companion's face. He rose once more. "I'll be happy to assist you in any way you require."

"May I see the post mortem report and hospital records?"

"Yes, I'll have them sent to you—where?"

"I'm at the Carlyle."

"Fine. Let me just think this over, then. Thanks for lunch. I'll be in touch."

Delia watched his retreating figure and suddenly felt one of those odd moments of being strangely off-balance. His 'I'll be in touch,' seemed to have a ring she didn't quite understand. And there hadn't been the usual struggle over the check that so many dreary men thought necessary to their virility.

As she lingered over the wine, Delia wondered

if it was too early in the day for cognac. Something in their conversation, something other than Magda's death had, she realized, disturbed her.

She glanced back at the now-empty chair opposite her and saw again Dr. Elliot's black eyes fixed upon her. A tremor ran through Delia then, the kind of deep physical response she rarely allowed to shake her frame. Catching Gerard's eye, she thought, *Foutre!* and ordered a double Courvoisier.

Chapter Seven

Adrift

Much to her amazement, Lady Delia Ross-Merlani found herself uncharacteristically early for a dinner date at Charlotte Maitland's. Fumbling for her set of Charlotte's keys in her handbag, she dropped some of the books topping the stack acquired at Rizzoli that afternoon. Bending down to collect the books, she inadvertently let go of her purse and watched helplessly as its contents spilled out all over the floor. *"Minchione!"* she hissed, crouching down.

Beginning to retrieve her things, she heard Charlotte's door opening behind her. Turning to greet her friend, Delia saw first a flash of metal streak past her vision and then felt the stunning blow to the side of her head. "How disappointing," she thought as she sank to the ground, "one really doesn't see stars." In the dance of colors that did fill her sight in those brief seconds, Delia remembered only seeing what she thought were wisps of red-brown lights. Then her eyes closed. . . .

She was in a punt on the Cam, floating lazily along with the currents. There were, she noticed, many boats on the river. But hers, she knew, could steer itself to safety, so she let her hand trail behind her in the cool water.

Suddenly a boat pulled up next to hers. In it sat a woman, the face obscured beneath a parasol. This punt was being poled by a big bronzed man. He turned his face to hers, and she recognized Ned Hennessey. "Ask me no more," he said.

And then just as suddenly, another boat like the first appeared on her other side. The bronze boatman turned again to her, but this time it was Jason Howland. "Ask me no more," he said.

And yet another boat appeared, Patrick Hennessey hailing her this time with the same words. A boat struck hers from behind, and she turned to face the bronze boatman, now Daniel Elliot. "Ask me no more," she heard him say.

Then the four boats, each piloted by the same protean image, each carrying the same shrouded passenger, encircled her boat, trapping her. All at once, the bells began to ring out from the colleges, pealing louder and louder still. The boats moved faster and faster, and she could hear the boatmen's repeated chant. "Ask me no more."

With a loud whoosh, all the parasols suddenly

flew up into the air, and the image of four exquisite Magdalenes swirled round her. "Magda!" she heard herself scream. "Magda!"

And in the growing whorl that pulled at her, Delia heard Magda's voice high above the bells: *Ask me no more. Ask me no more.*

"Magda!" Delia screamed again. But she was answered now only by the distant sound of her own fear. . . .

Someone was calling her name then, echoing down a long tunnel. *Deeeliaaaa.* She felt cool water on her temples, and the sound ceased to resonate. *Delia. Delia.* She looked up into the liquid brown pools of Charlotte Maitland's eyes.

"Charley," Delia said, but the sound seemed to come from outside her body.

"Don't move, I'll get a doctor."

"No, Charley. Wait! I'm all right. Really I am. Please." Something in Delia's tone, something other than her usual imperviousness, made Charlotte pause. "Just help me up, Charley."

Charlotte helped her friend to her feet and inside onto the couch. At Delia's direction, she brought an ice pack and some brandy.

Gingerly feeling her head, Delia said, "Oh, a nasty bump, that."

"What happened?"

"I don't quite know," Delia said, taking an unladylike swig of brandy followed by another. "I got here rather early, and someone coshed me on the head. It *does* pay to be tardy, I believe.

Where are my things?"

Charlotte hastily returned to the hallway and collected her friend's books, the two Valentino boxes, one parcel from Porthault, and the handbag, having first gathered up the contents from the floor. She handed this last to Delia, who immediately went through her possessions.

"Anything amiss?" Charlotte asked.

Delia began to shake her head, felt a sharp flash of pain and thought better of the gesture. "No, nothing. I have several hundred dollars in cash, credit cards and my Chopard watch which reads"—here she shook it—"approximately two o'clock." The two women exchanged smiles. Delia possessed many expensive and beautiful timepieces, and although she generally had one about her person, it was common knowledge among her near and dear that it was rarely looked at or to.

"Well, certainly no thief could have missed those," Charlotte said. "Your wallet and watch were right out on the floor."

Delia frowned and took another deep swallow of brandy. "The gentleman came out of your door, Charley. Was it unlocked?" Charlotte shook her head. "Any sign of someone having broken in?" Again a negative. "Take a look around and see if anything has been disturbed or is missing."

"Shouldn't we call the police?"

"No," Delia said firmly, "first see what's

61

what."

Charlotte made a cursory tour of her rooms and returned to her friend. "Nothing appears to have been touched."

Delia thought for a moment and asked, "What happened to Magda's wedding band — she did have one, didn't she? White gold, wasn't it?"

"Oh, yes, she had one. It was quite lovely actually. Not gold — platinum. Ned has a matching band. I don't know where Magda's is. She wasn't wearing it . . . when she died. I expect it's at Jason's with her things. I've gotten some of her belongings already — books mostly. I'm going back over there tomorrow to collect the rest. Why?"

Delia took the ice pack from her head and began to tuck stray strands back into her chignon. "No reason — just thought I saw a band like hers today." Then quietly she asked, "Charley, who has keys to this flat?"

"Well, you do and Magda did."

"Do me a favor — no questions please — when you're at Jason's tomorrow, take especial care to see if Magda's set of keys is with her things. Don't ask Jason, just make a careful search."

"You don't think Jason. . . ?"

"No," Delia said, "I don't think Jason was here today."

"Delia, I do think we should call the police."

Delia took her compact from her bag and began meticulous repairs to her makeup. "No, Charley."

"Shouldn't we call a locksmith to change the lock?"

Delia looked up sharply. "No. Most emphatically not. Our 'prowler' meant no harm to anyone, I think."

"Meant no harm? Delia, he struck you on the head."

"He was startled. I'll take more care next time."

"Next time?"

"Yes, Charley. Now, don't fret. There's no real danger—truly. Call Mr. and Mrs. Mac and have them bring some goodies by for dinner. I don't feel like dining out." Her significant look propelled her friend to the phone.

As Charlotte set to her task, Delia tried to compose her scattered recollections. She didn't know how long she had sat thinking when Charlotte's voice broke into her thoughts.

"Ask you what?" Delia looked up in bewilderment. "You were murmuring something like 'ask me' as you regained consciousness, and you were repeating it again just now."

With some effort, Delia took up all the skeins of her thoughts and tried to recognize the pattern. "Ask me," she said slowly, "no more. Yes, that's it. Ask me no more."

"Isn't that the title of a poem?" Charlotte asked after a moment.

"Oh, is it?" Delia asked slowly.

"I think so. Yes . . . wait . . . you know how

Magda was always reciting poetry for us." Delia nodded. Charlotte's voice took on a wistful tone. "At the times I was *most* exasperated with her, Mags would quote some lines from oh, Mallarme, Ovid, William Carlos Williams . . . and I would instantly forgive her." Delia's face, she knew, mirrored Charlotte's sad smile.

"Anyway, the two of us were in Cambridge that last term, and Magda had come to visit. We took a punt out on the river—remember? We were talking about this being our final weeks at university and how we didn't really know what we planned to do."

"And I said," Delia broke in breathlessly, suddenly focusing on the memory, " 'Ask me no more questions about the future.' "

"Then Magda recited a poem . . . do you remember the poet?"

"Tennyson," Delia put in, "Alfred, Lord Tennyson."

"Right!"

"Do you have a copy of his poems?"

"Oh, yes, surely," Charlotte said, going to her bookcase, "Magda gave me so many collected works as gifts." She found the volume, flipped through it and said, "Here it is." At Delia's nod, she began to read aloud:

> " 'Ask me no more: thy fate and
>   mine are seal'd:
> I strove against the stream and all

64

in vain:
Let the great river take me to
    the main:
No more, dear love, for at a
    touch I yield;
Ask me no more.' "

Delia listened to her friend's voice and heard the sad beseeching tones of the elder sister in it. A kind of chill, a shudder, ran through her then, and she sank back in her seat.

"Delia?" Charlotte said, her voice full of concern. "Are you all right—do you feel dizzy again or ill? I'll fetch a doctor."

Delia held out her hand, and Charlotte grasped it. Delia's hand was icy cold as she stared out now into middle distance. "Charley, I've had the most peculiar sense. It's like a premonition . . . but in reverse."

"What, Delia? I'm afraid I don't quite—"

"Charley?"

"Yes, Delia."

"Charley, do you know what I think? I think that this is all about the questions *we aren't supposed to ask*. I think there is one simple answer." Delia looked up at her friend and said, *"Magda was murdered!"*

Charlotte sat down next to Delia. "Murdered?"

"I don't know how, certainly, or why, or by whom. But I feel this deep, deep in my being. Magda lived her life and died as she lived. She 'strove against the stream and all in vain.' Charley . . . someone *mur*dered your sister."

Charlotte put her head against her friend's shoulder and let it rest there. Without a word, she accepted Delia's conclusion as she had accepted and learned to rely on Delia's greater insight all her life. "Delia?"

Delia put an arm about Charlotte's waist. "Yes, Charley. I will. I will." And they sat thus for some time and only arose when the Mac-Phees tapped loudly at the door bringing dinner.

Chapter Eight

Stalking Prey

Before she pushed the elevator button in Daniel Elliot's building, Delia looked in the mirror to inspect her armor one last time. It wasn't really a beautiful face, she knew. Her eyes were good, arresting—but her lips were too full, her brows too prominent, her nose too aggressive. She had inherited Papa's sallow Italian complexion and not Adela's English bloom. Now as her tan faded, she feared she looked yellowed, wilted. The taupe cloche on her head did make her look pinched, she suddenly decided, instead of precious. Well, at least the Louis Féraud suit looked nice—a bit dark—well no, distinguished.

Delia sighed. She had always envied Magda's delicate blond beauty, and even Charlotte's gamine good looks seemed superior to her own right now. Deciding that a different shade of lip gloss would not help, she angrily snapped her compact shut and pushed the elevator button.

Delia was not completely happy about visiting

Dr. Daniel Elliot at his apartment. The medical examiner had sent along one of those infernal Post-Its stuck to Magda's post mortem report. His brief note stated that he wished to discuss the Hennessey case and gave the time and the place for this meeting. Delia knew she would have felt more comfortable if they had met on more neutral turf. The daughter of Signor Federico Merlani and the Countess of Ross had been taught never to be quite happy about situations over which she was not absolute mistress.

Delia knocked on the door to Daniel Elliot's apartment and waited, impatiently tapping her foot. Although rarely on time herself, her ladyship simply loathed others being late.

After several moments, she knocked again, this time loud distinctive raps. No answer. Delia checked the message from Daniel Elliot and verified the address, date and time as correct.

She knocked again, an ember of anger flaring full at the silence within. Digging into her purse, she found pen and paper and began to compose a stinging note, which included references in four languages, two of them considered quite dead and particularly obscure.

She was, however, interrupted in this pleasurable effort by the sight of Daniel Elliot jogging down the hall toward her. He was dressed in running shoes, shorts and a tee shirt that read "Property of Johns Hopkins University." He was red-faced and gleaming with sweat. Her hasty perusal of him showed a quantity of red-blond hair on sleek, muscular legs. This unaccountably pleased Delia and made her flush slightly before she quickly returned her gaze to his face.

Daniel smiled at her. "Glad you could make it."

No apology. No explanation. Not even, "I was out running and lost track of the time." Delia's face remained stony, but her host appeared oblivious as he let her in.

"Make yourself at home. I'm going to take a quick shower."

Left alone in his living room, Delia gave vent to her annoyance by stamping her Maraolo pump on the unassuming Rya rug. Inspecting the room, she noted with a sniff the simple utilitarian furniture arranged with little art or taste. She began to feel a bit better as Daniel Elliot, in her estimation, appeared a bit worse.

"Have some wine," came Daniel's voice from the next room.

It was only then that Delia noticed the ice bucket with the familiar green-flowered champagne bottle. She poured a glass for herself and sipped thoughtfully.

"Put on some music," the disembodied voice then commanded from the shower.

Delia was surprised to find an impressive collection of Renaissance, Baroque and Classical CDs. Finding a particular favorite, she put it on and listened attentively to the music.

When Daniel Elliot emerged, his hair still damp, dressed in jeans and another Hopkins tee shirt, he startled Delia out of that reverie that music always put her in. He looked younger, more boyish she thought. Suddenly a swift pang of some nearly forgotten sense filled her, and Delia hastily thrust the feeling away.

Daniel refilled her glass and poured champagne for himself. "Got your brand right, didn't I?" he asked, referring to the bottle in his hand.

"Yes," she replied and all at once forgave him his earlier rudeness.

"Book One is my favorite," he said and for a moment Delia couldn't place his remark in context.

"The Bach? Oh, yes, *The Well-Tempered Clavier* is quite fine."

"And Marlowe plays to perfection," he commented as they listened together to the music.

"She was marvelous. Extraordinary," Delia said wistfully, her voice starting to catch unexpectedly in her throat. "I miss her dreadfully sometimes."

"You knew Sylvia Marlowe?" he asked.

"Oh, yes. She was my teacher . . . and my friend for many years."

"Do you still play?"

"Yes, when I can. I have an instrument at home in Surrey and one at my flat in London."

"Only *two* residences? 'Three addresses always inspires confidence, even in tradesmen.' "

She laughed at his attempted imitation of Lady Bracknell and was instantly charmed by this unexpected display of literary wit. "Actually, I've been considering a *pied à terre* here in New York. To stay close to Charley . . . Ms. Maitland . . . for a time."

70

He nodded. "Can you tell me a bit about Magda Hennessey, something of her background and habits? I'd like to have a clearer sense of her before we begin."

"Begin what?"

"The investigation into the last months of her life."

"How does one begin an investigation?"

"By getting to know the cast of characters. I need more information on your friend before we start."

Delia was acutely aware of the first person plural Dr. Elliot was now bandying about. Regretting the very short and tight linen skirt that prevented her from pulling her legs up under her, Delia perched somewhat uncomfortably on the couch.

"Well, all right. Here are the facts, Doctor. Magda and Charlotte's parents were Czech Jews who came to London just before the war. Mr. Maracek changed the family name to Maitland—so English you see—and ran a highly successful fur import business. When Magda was twelve and Charlotte ten, both parents were killed in a car crash. Since they had no relations, most had perished in the camps, the court-appointed guardian sent the girls off to school. That's where we met.

"Both Charley and I took our degrees at Cambridge. Mine is in Medieval Studies, as I have said. Charley took hers in Botany." She saw the beginnings of a smile and acknowledged it with one of her own. "Yes, it does fit her. There is something rather flowerlike about Charley. She is someone who only opens slowly to people, but then can blaze out in full color when she does." Delia heard how charged her voice had become and with some effort returned to a more professional manner.

"While we were at school, Mags—that is, Magda—moved to the States to study Art History at Radcliffe. She met Ned, Edward Hennessey, in her senior year. He was just finishing up his Ph.D. in History at Harvard. They were married about a year later. Ned got a post at Columbia, and they moved to New York . . . in . . . let me see . . . 1988 . . . yes, 1988—I was at Harvard in '89."

"What were you doing at Harvard?" Daniel asked.

"My husband was from Boston and we lived there for a short while."

"Your husband?" he asked quickly.

Delia waved this question aside and dismissed any discussion of Theo much as she had the actual man two years before. "You know it was rather a peculiar marriage from the start—Magda and Ned's, that is. At first, Magda was passionately devoted to Ned. She gave up her former friends and seemed to throw herself into being the dutiful professor's wife." Delia frowned and took a sip of the champagne. "Charley and I were really quite astonished."

"At the change in Magda?"

Delia shook her head, felt the constriction of the hat and took it off. Her fingers idly tucked in the strands that had strayed from her chignon as she sat momentarily lost in thought. "Oh, no. Magda was like a chameleon—could take on any colors she wished. And often did. We knew she would tire of this routine in time and look for new amusements. No, what puzzled us was Ned's unswerving devotion to Magda. He's so rigid, so stolid. Long after Mags was up to her old tricks, he still and absolutely refused to let her go. His stoical acceptance of her was awesome and in many ways inexplicable.

"Once, Magda disappeared for several weeks, and Ned hired a private detective to find her—I haven't a clue as to what led her there and neither did Charley—but Magda ended up in San Francisco working in a rather posh brothel. Very drunk, Charley said. Ned flew out there, brought her back, put her in Payne Whitney and remained lovingly at her side till she was once more in the pink."

"Very touching," Daniel said, his voice even.

"Oh, no, it was oppressive. I think Magda was always trying to escape her husband by more and more outrageous behavior. But Ned always took her back, cared for her—no matter what."

"Why, do you suppose?"

"I don't know, really, but I've had a theory for quite some time. Ned, you see, came from a poor Boston Irish family—no, it's not what you might imagine. He didn't care about Magda's money—although there's heaps, I shouldn't wonder. But I think Ned Hennessey saw Magdalene Maitland as a kind of treasure. Magda was exquisitely beautiful—you should have seen her when she was alive—she was ethereal, remote. I believe Ned felt he had captured this extraordinary thing—this creature so outside his ken—and he meant to keep it—at whatever cost."

"But he did let her go," Daniel interrupted. "I mean, she was living with someone else at the time of her death."

Delia sat for a moment quietly twirling errant strands of hair in her characteristic gesture of concentration. "Well, yes. But she'd left him before, you see. This time, however, he does seem to have quietly stepped aside. Another piece that doesn't quite fit," she murmured.

"Couldn't he finally have given up?" Daniel asked. "She was lovely, as you say, but couldn't he just have gotten fed up and said 'The hell with her'?"

Delia heard once again Ned's voice proclaiming, "I *am* Magda's husband." "No," she said, "it's completely out of character. He would never have let Magda go. Not finally. His life's mission, I think, was to possess her. No matter what. No matter how."

There was a silence as their words hung in the air, heavy, clouded, dense. The pair, intent on their conversation, had not noticed the gathering shadows of the evening. Delia's eyes suddenly met his, but Daniel did not rise to put on the light or break the spell suddenly palpable between them.

As they sat sipping the last of the champagne, Delia became aware of a subtle shift in the tension. Daniel's look was still intense, but it did not hold the same note as before. When they had been speaking of Magda, his face had been full of inquiry. Now his gaze seemed to be going beyond her features and back, back into her very recesses.

Delia sat up then and attempted rather primly to pull her skirt down over her knees. She spoke next in her most boarding school English accent. "I'm most especially grateful for your help in this, Dr. Elliot."

"Daniel," he said, his eyes never leaving her.

"Yes, Daniel. Well, I shall begin by speaking with Charlotte, Jason, and some of Magda's friends. Perhaps I can get some ideas . . . leads . . . right, leads . . ." her voice trailed off.

Daniel put his glass down on the table, and she noticed his strong, elegant hands. Suddenly Delia stood up; as an expert rider she was now alert to this immediate danger. She quickly began to put her hat on and could sense him wordlessly watching her every move.

"Thank you for the wine, Doctor . . . uh . . . Daniel. I'm touched by your thoughtfulness . . . I mean, the champagne. I imagine my having a 'brand' as you call it may seem a mite pretentious. But once, you see, I was walking with Papa down the Calle del Paradiso . . . oh, that's in Venice which is his family home. We passed a shop that had many bright green bottles in the window. I was only about eight . . . and well . . . I began to clap my hands in delight pointing at the one with all the flowers on it. Papa went right in then and bought a bottle for me. It was my very first grown-up gift from him. And I have always drunk Perrier-Jouët since. It is rather silly, I do know, but some things we have from childhood stay with us, don't they? Well, in any case—oh, yes, isn't that an apt turn of phrase?—thanks once again and I'll be sure to ring your office just as soon as I learn anything." Feeling tremendously like the foolish schoolgirl she knew she sounded, Delia hastily crossed to the door. She felt, rather than saw, Daniel spring to his feet and follow her.

His hand closed over hers on the knob. "I have two tickets for the Waverly Consort on Saturday night. Will you join me?"

Delia stood stock still, her heart absurdly loud in her chest. Admonishing herself, Delia turned to Daniel Elliot and opened her mouth to give her best garden-party assent when his lips came down on her own.

His kiss surprised her; it was long and cool, not the red impassioned thrust she had imagined it would be. Then he stood apart and wordlessly let her leave.

Outside his door, Delia took a few moments to catch her breath; she was panting as if from a chase. Stepping into the elevator, her eyes began to narrow in anger. Oh, yes! She knew bloody well why Daniel Elliot had summoned her into his presence. Oh, indeed. And Lady Delia Ross-Merlani recognized and catalogued that for safety's sake; when next she and Daniel Elliot met, it would be on her own carefully chosen time and territory.

Chapter Nine

Riding Forth

"God, I feel awful."

"You look like shit."

"Oh, thanks ever so much. If there was one thing I absolutely needed to add to this absolutely lousy day, it was one of your compliments." Daniel Elliot ran his hand through his hair, brushing it off his forehead. Then he sneezed.

"Sounds to me like you're coming down with a cold, Doctor."

"And thanks ever so much for the ingenious diagnosis," he said. Then he blew his nose.

Linda Elliot's black eyes stared long and hard at her older brother's face. "But you know, you look crappier than just a cold. How come your day was so lousy?"

Daniel kicked off his sneakers and put his feet up on the coffee table. "I'm swamped with work."

"So?"

"And I don't seem to have the stick-to-it-iveness to get through it."

"Really? You must be sick, then. You're usually such a paragon of perseverance when it comes to your career."

Daniel shook his head. "It's all becoming so dull, so routine."

"You're too smart for your own good, know that, Danny?" She got up and refreshed the scotch in their glasses. "Mom says you should get married."

"Mom says *you* should get married. Marriage—universal panacea." Daniel drummed his fingers on his leg for a minute. "I've met a woman."

His sister again gave him the once over. "Oh? A woman? From the symptoms it seems more like what Watson called *the woman*."

"Lady Delia Ross-Merlani," he murmured thoughtfully, not attending to his sister's words.

"Yummy name. Sounds like a thoroughbred."

At that, Daniel gave a rueful smile. "Why didn't *I* think of that?"

"What's the lady like?"

"She's an odd mix, really. One minute, she comes on like the Queen of Sheba, the next minute she's the girl next door." Daniel grinned at his sister's skeptical look. "Well, if you live next door to Windsor Castle, I guess."

"Is she beautiful or just one of the beautiful people?"

"Actually, neither—although she definitely runs with quite a crowd." He briefly explained how he came to lunch with Delia Ross-Merlani.

"She does sound a bit out of your league,

78

Danny. I should think that blue blood might be a bit too cool for you."

Daniel considered this and recognized something of the wisdom in his sister's words. "Oh, fuck it! I'm tired of those bright, earthy, Sarah Lawrence types that keep coming my way."

Linda paused and said, "Sure your interest in this 'Lady' isn't simply a reaction to Robin? After all, an English peeress is a far cry from a Jewish princess."

"I don't know," Daniel said irritably. He got up and began to rifle through his CD collection. "Something about her," he said in an altered tone of voice, now avoiding his sister's eyes, "really bugs me." Then he sneezed again.

"Perhaps," Linda said, "you're confusing being bitten by the love bug with the flu bug."

Daniel opened his mouth to reply when another sneeze seemed fortuitously to prove his sister's point. With a shrug of resignation, he finished off the scotch, kissed her on the forehead and took himself off to bed.

"God, I feel good."

"You look tired."

"Tired, but good," Delia said as she walked through the suite, tossing her things around. She felt as if some elemental spark seemed to have been rekindled in her over the past few days. She now wanted to reclaim sovereignty over her body, mind and future. To this end, Delia had begun with what she called "the basics": getting back in shape by taking a vigorous exercise class for an hour and a half each morning. Sore and sweaty though it left her, Delia emerged from the exercise studio each day triumphant.

There were also several tantalizing problems to coax her mind out of its nearly year-long hibernation. These she only vaguely identified under the headings: "Magda Maitland," "Ned Hennessey" and "Dr. Daniel Elliot." The questions of the future she had decided to leave to settle themselves.

"A cup of tea?" Mrs. MacPhee inquired as she gathered up the discarded leotard, tights and towel from where each had landed about the suite.

"Yes, *mia cara*, sounds just the ticket."

In an instant, Mrs. MacPhee produced a tea cart laden with a freshly brewed pot of Lapsang Souchong, scones, butter and jam.

Delia nibbled a scone. "Deeeelish—wherever did you get these on this side of the globe?"

"Mrs. Dillingham's cook sent them over especially for you."

"Really? Oh, yum. How nice to know that porky ole Agatha Dillingham is good for something other than taking up space in one's drawing room." Mrs. MacPhee shot her a disapproving look, and Delia dutifully lowered her eyes and looked a contrition she did not feel. "Where's the mister?"

"Out fetching those things you ordered from Erno Laszlo."

Delia sipped her tea. "I'd love a bath and then, I

80

think, a nap. I'm dining out *ce soir.*"

"A lot of dashing about lately," Mrs. MacPhee said evenly. Delia recognized this note as an introduction and simply nodded. "New clothes, makeup, classes, dinners, dates. What's it all about, then?"

"I'm having, I think, a renascence, appropriately enough."

"So it seems. Why?"

Delia stretched. "I feel as if I've shed an old skin, somehow. Ennui, I imagine. I now have something to do." Mrs. MacPhee said nothing, but her look made Delia go on. "There's something about Magda's last months that seems all awry. I can't quite put my finger on it, but I'm trying to find out just what."

"Because you haven't anything better to do?"

Delia considered this and then slowly shook her head. "No. It might have been that way at first, but not now. I suddenly want very much to understand what happened to Magdalene. It's almost as if I feel something has me vaguely connected to her still, something more than my relationship with her—whatever it actually was—and my love for Charlotte."

Mrs. MacPhee nodded. "Well, whatever it is that's got you moving, I'm glad for it. I don't care what you do, Miss Delia, as long as you're *doing* something."

Delia listened to this last and then said, "Adela is always doing something, though, isn't she? And you don't much approve of her life."

Mrs. MacPhee did not deny this latter assertion which had long been a bond between them. "Your mother is always *going* somewhere. There's a great difference in that. Someday," Mrs. MacPhee said, as she brushed the hair off Delia's face, "Lady Ross may see that she really is going nowhere at all."

"Perhaps that's what she needs to make her happy," Delia said softly.

"No," Mrs. MacPhee said with conviction. "She just keeps moving—and always has kept moving—so she doesn't have to face how unhappy she truly is."

After a long pause Delia finally said, "She loved Papa very much, didn't she?"

Mrs. MacPhee paused, looked over at Delia and then shook her head. "You're using the wrong tense, my gel."

Delia opened her mouth again but was interrupted by the sound of the buzzer. Mrs. MacPhee returned with a letter which she slit open and handed to Delia.

Inside were two tickets for the Waverly Consort and a brief note. This, Delia noted, had no salutation, betraying the writer's uncertainty at exactly how to address her.

Been battling a bug for the last few days and am now vanquished. My personal physician, though a jerk in some ways, seems to be right about one thing: Every time I get up I fall down. This seems to be a deterrent to a big night on the town. In lieu of that, I'm taking a hot bath and a bottle of booze. Hope you enjoy the concert and will accept this note as a raincheck for dinner.

Daniel Elliot

"Mrs. Mac," Delia said thoughtfully, "do we have such a thing as a local phone directory?"

"I suppose," she said, eyeing Delia carefully. Going over to the bedside bureau, she fetched the requested item and handed it to her mistress.

"Thanks muchly. Be a darling and run a bath, would you?"

Delia sat cross-legged upon the bed and planted the phone in front of her. First she called Charlotte, who gratefully accepted the tickets for "Totally Telemann." Charlotte said she would ask Jason to join her. Delia, surprised, lifted a brow, though she said nothing to her friend. But she made a mental note to keep an eye on Charlotte and Jason. "Rebound, grieving and that sort of nonsense. Not quite the thing to begin a love affair. And Charley *is* such a dolt about men," she thought.

For the next fifteen minutes, her ladyship let her fingers do the dancing. Presently, her list was complete. Just before she stepped into the steaming, scented water, she gave instructions to Mrs. MacPhee. "Tell Mr. Mac to bring these tickets to Charley Maitland and then come back here to fetch me. We'll have several errands to run this afternoon."

"Will you still be going out this evening, Miss Delia?"

"Ah, yes," she said, slipping in up to her neck. "I'm going to the bedside of a sick friend, Mrs. Mac."

"How virtuous of you, Miss Delia," Mrs. Mac-Phee replied dryly.

"Ah virtue, Mrs. Mac, will, I trust, have nothing whatsoever to do with it."

Splashing about, Delia smiled to herself. *Mais oui!* The reins were once more in her hands, she knew. But an expert rider, she recognized that bringing this particular mount to bay would be a challenge worthy of her talents, equestrian and otherwise.

Chapter Ten

Wine and Roses

Daniel Elliot appeared quite robust to Delia Ross-Merlani as he peered out into the hallway at her. The flush that rose to his face came not from fever, she saw, but surprise.

"Good evening," she said. "I am the proverbial mountain to Mohammed." He looked at her for a moment, puzzled. "First things first," she said briskly, "you get back into bed immediately." And with that, Delia walked past him into the apartment, put several bundles down in the living room and began to make herself at home in the tiny kitchen. Daniel followed her. Turning a frosty eye upon him, she said, "Back into bed, sir," her voice regal. With a soft cough and smile, the doctor did as instructed.

Delia went over to the stereo and put on one of the CDs she had brought. Then she went into the bedroom. This, she noted, was decorated with the same haphazard bad taste—although she did appreciate the handsome bookcase and large brass bed.

"Telemann?" he asked.

"Tonight 'Totally Telemann.' A slight change in program; this is the Colegium Aureum playing."

"Concerto in D Major," he said smiling.

She nodded approvingly and realized just then she'd somehow assumed this same taste in music. But she did not pause to question the significance of this assumption. "Now, you stay put while I bring you some victuals. Keep your strength up and all that," she said.

"Victuals?"

Delia ignored his query and asked, "Do you have any vases?"

"Vases? No, but there are several large jars in the cabinet above the refrigerator. What exactly are we eating?" he asked, his smile widening. Delia again ignored his question and left the room.

She returned several minutes later, carrying a jar brimming with flowers. There was an amazing array of cymbidium and dendrobium orchids, birds of paradise and calla lilies—all of these punctuated by huge deep-pink damask roses. The scent of old roses swiftly filled the room.

She said, "To delight and refresh the senses." He sniffed through clogged nostrils. "Olfactory and otherwise." Then she quickly left the room once again.

When she returned, Delia was carrying a large tray which she placed on the bed in front of Daniel. She ticked off the items before him. "Our friend Gerard at Olympe sends his warmest wishes and best Beluga caviar. *Potage de poulet* from Stein's Deli on West 72nd, blini in sour cream sauce from my chum Antoine at The Russian Tea Room. And if you are very good and finish all of this, I have wangled us two pieces of perfect pecan pie from an old friend at The Coach House."

"Do all of your friends work in four-star restaurants?" he asked, accepting a Bath Oliver cracker slathered with caviar. She smiled, but did not rise to the bait. "Tell me," he continued, "did you learn the medicinal secrets of *potage du poulet* at your mother's knee?"

"Actually, Mrs. MacPhee née Stewart of Nairn, Scotland, who is my aide de camp, swears that the clans have been downing chicken soup for many a year to ward off the chill of the firth air," Delia said, delivering this in a perfect Scots burr.

"That's very comforting. Her sentiments are in complete agreement with those of Mrs. Elliot, née Lansky of Minsk, Russia, and Sheepshead Bay, Brooklyn, my mother."

"Ah *bellissimo*," Delia said. "Telemann's Concerto No. 6 in A Minor—perfect accompaniment to a grand meal."

As he lifted his spoon to tackle the soup, Daniel paused and asked, "Aren't you joining me?"

Once again she disappeared and returned with the ice bucket, a bottle of Perrier-Jouët champagne and a large pastrami and corned beef sandwich on rye.

"Isn't that rather plebian fare," Daniel said motioning toward her plate, "with such patrician swill."

"Dave Stein himself, I will have you know, made me a gift of this sandwich upon making my acquaintance this very evening."

"Another culinary notch on your gunbelt?"

"Eat!" she commanded, "and be silent."

After several moments Daniel said, "It must be something genetic. Passed along from one generation to another among Jewish women. And finally a vestige of this trait has come to rest in as unlikely a personage as that of Professor Lady Ms. Delia Ross-Merlani."

Delia daintily swallowed down another bite of pastrami and then took a hefty pull of the Perrier-Jouët before she said in her best upper-crust tones, "Do go on. Anthropology is *so* broadening."

"Well, my extensive researches have shown that the first thing a Jewish woman thinks of when confronted by a man is to get him to eat."

Again Delia drank some wine, carefully considering her next move. Then she said, "Actually, that's not the first thing I thought of when first confronted by you."

"Oh?" Daniel asked, a blini poised before his mouth.

Delia tilted her head to the side and studied him once again. "No, Doctor. Not at all. Truth to tell,

I was trying to picture precisely how you would look in exactly the place you are right now."

They continued eating for several minutes in silence, and then, almost as if on cue, both put their plates aside. Daniel got out of bed and stood for a moment before the waiting woman.

"Take your damn hat off," he said at last. Delia pulled the long sharp pin out, took off her hat, pushed the pin slowly back in and flung the hat off into a corner of the room. It landed squashing its crown.

Daniel ran his long fingers through her hair, found the combs holding it in place, removed them and tossed them aside. These landed in opposite corners of the room. Then he watched as she shook out the long tresses. Delia then reached down and took off her high-heel pumps; she handed one to Daniel. Almost in unison, they each pitched a shoe in long overhand arcs into the far recesses of the room.

Delia waited in the silence that followed and felt a curious sense of suspension. She knew herself to be on the edge of a moment of something of significance in her life. Daniel took her face between his hands and looked once more into her eyes. No word or gesture between them, she responded instead as if this were the next movement in a ballet combination—without words, without thought—wholly totally in her viscera: Delia swung her head forward, allowing her hair to tumble across his shoulders. Daniel put his lips to her nape and drew her to him. His lips moved along the curve till they reached the hollow in the blade. Then Daniel paused, and gazed at her once more. Delia closed her eyes and, in an uncharacteristic moment of surrender, allowed him to lift her up; she knew herself placed ever so gently but surely across the bed.

Forever after, whenever Daniel Elliot made love to her, no matter where they were or when it was, Delia would always imagine she could hear the soft strains of Telemann and smell the heady scent of old roses as his lips began each time their descent from the nape of her neck.

Chapter Eleven

Before and After

"Why did you marry him?"

It was tenish the next morning, and the couple was polishing off the last of their communally prepared breakfast: caviar omelet, black coffee and the pecan pie they hadn't quite gotten to the night before. They were sitting naked, opposite each other, fresh from a long night of lovemaking and a brisk, erotic shower.

Delia studied Daniel's long, lean body with a now-unabashed appreciative gaze. "How old are you?" she asked without removing her eyes from his torso.

"Thirty-six." And then, unembarrassed, he answered her unspoken question. "I swim at least a mile three times a week, and run daily. Usually keeps me healthy as well as in shape," he said. "I must say, though, most of my flu seems gone this morning. It's either the dish of soup I had last night or the super dish I had all night long." She groaned. "Sorry—bad jokes, you will find, are my tragic flaw."

"You do seem quite recovered," Delia said pointedly, "considering the *severity* of your recent illness."

Daniel flushed and shifted uncomfortably in his seat. "Well, I wasn't all that sick. It was really more a case of cold feet than cold."

"I see," Delia said. "I wondered at that." Her voice softened. "I certainly appreciate your candor, Daniel."

"Touché?"

"Touché," she said.

"Now, where were we? Ah yes, we were talking about Mr. Morgan."

"No, *we* weren't. You asked . . . well, never mind. Why did I marry Theo? Oh, I don't know really," she said, stretching her arms in a long yawn, her small breasts arching up.

"Yes, you do," Daniel said.

"Yes, I do," Delia replied. "Let's see . . . I had just finished up my degree at Cambridge. Met him at a party . . . *attraente* . . . stock analyst . . . Bostonian . . . old money . . . anyway, I liked him, liked even more his sister, his parents, his silver-haired grandparents, hearth and home. They're a tight-knit bunch, the Morgans. And I thought sitting down to family dinner with them would be a little bit of heaven. Some people marry for family connections. In my case, it was making connection with a family."

"What happened?"

"Theo bored me. I bored myself . . . I don't know," she said, her voice suddenly irritable.

Daniel leaned forward a bit in his seat and briefly put his hands upon her thin shoulders. "Yes, you do," he said.

"Yes, I do," Delia said, meeting his gaze. "He was a sweet man, but I never really loved him or ever pretended to. He loved me, I think. I believe I hurt him very much. But I know now that I won't ever take anyone's love for granted again. You see, the Morgan part was what attracted me to Theodore Morgan."

"What about your family?"

"My family?" Delia gave a hearty laugh which rang a false note to his ears. "Well, let's see. Adela, *ma mere,* stayed with Papa about fifteen minutes after I was born. They were actually both delighted to go their several ways. Adela was, and is, far more interested in 'being seen' than in seeing anything or anyone. The only real interest Papa has is the kind that accrues. It's all very civilized, don'tcha know. At first, I trooped about with Adela for a time—taken care of by the Mac-Phees—until my boarding school years. There I met Charley and Magda . . . bona fide orphans . . . and we became friends. Marrying Theo was my experiment in family living. It looked like a Norman Rockwell cover. But had about as much depth, I soon learned."

"You sound bitter."

"No, just disappointed. Very few things in my life ever live up to my anticipations." She reached

93

across, took his hand and kissed the palm. "You're one of the very first."

Daniel took her face between his hands and gently kissed her. Although expected, there was still something of a shock to her system in the coolness of his lips. "Where do you live now?" he asked when she was once more settled in her chair.

"Live? I live anywhere . . . everywhere . . . nowhere, really." She frowned as she remembered Mrs. MacPhee's assessment of her mother's life. "I have a flat in London as I've said. And I often go down to Adela's estate, Rosemuir . . . that's near Haslemere in Surrey."

"Your mother is . . . Lady Merlani?"

Delia shook her head. "The Merlani is from my father." She gave a little shy laugh. "The name means whiting—the fish, you see. The Merlanis were fishermen in Venice way back when. My great-great-grandfather, a shrewd character, acquired several boats and became quite successful. The family enterprises took off from there. Papa's holdings are vast, world-wide. And he rules them—and everyone—like a feudal lord."

"And your mother?"

"My mother is the Countess of Ross, a peeress in her own right. The Ross earldom descends in the female line. Might call her actually the Peeress Jewess—it's quite a story really." She looked over at Daniel and at his nod continued. "Well, back in the thirteenth and fourteenth centuries, it was fashionable for Scots of some position—though not of the nobility, you see—to send their sons to

94

Venice to be educated. Mostly to study medicine. The sciences were flourishing in La Serenissima. They were all so very enlightened back then that they herded all the Jews into one area to live, an area called Ghetto. That's where the English word comes from. Anyway—the Ghetto was known as a place of some culture, and because it was closed off each night, it acquired an extra patina of interest to many young men. A number of these fell in love with the dark-eyed, and one imagines, rather exotic Jewesses and brought them back to Edinburgh. Which is how one finds so many dark-eyed Scottish Jews living there even today.

"It seems that one of these young men—of a minor branch of the Ross clan—brought home just such a bride . . . and the children, of course, took the religion of their mother. That much is historical fact. The rest, I think, gets a bit murky with historical myth, legend and downright lying. During the time of that business with Bonny Prince Charlie, the Ross family managed to do some service—spying I would guess—for the Crown and were rewarded with an earldom. I'm not entirely sure how it came to be descended in the female line—the records merely show the earldom being bestowed on the family. But descend it does through us womenfolk. Thus we have Adela, the Countess of Ross."

"So you are in fact descended on both sides from Venetians."

"Technically that's so. But Adela is so thoroughly an English rose that you mightn't even suggest it. A right Tory is what she is."

"Your father doesn't still live in Venice?"

"No—though most of the Merlani family is still there. I've quite a group of terribly Catholic cousins—rich, arrogant, and very thin-blooded and -skinned. I like them even less than the bunches of Adela's poor relations—of which there are many. You must know the type—poor but oh, so genteel. Really, my whole family is like something out of one of those Gothic novels that young girls read in private during Victorian times. I've even a great-aunt secreted away in a convent in Venice—Sister Annunziata—can you imagine that?"

Daniel smiled. "Quite frankly—no. Sounds like a bad soap opera to me. Where does your father live?"

"In Milan, mostly. He has a villa on Lake Como, flats in Rome, Paris, London et cetera. I don't visit with him too often," Delia said, avoiding Daniel's eye as she studied nonexistent flaws in her pedicure. Finally she looked up brightly and asked, "And you? Never taken the plunge?" He shook his head. "No near misses?"

His face clouded over. "Yes, one. Robin."

Delia gave a slight shake of her shoulders. Robin! Oh, God, how she loathed precious names. She disliked this Robin instantly. "What happened? And don't say you don't know, because you do."

"Yes, I do. We were together a couple of years. Everything was fine. She was bright, clever, good in bed, lovely out. And my family adored her."

"Your family?"

"My parents—still live in Brooklyn. I have two sisters: Rachel—married, two kids in Lawrence—"

"Who's Lawrence?"

He laughed. "You have an odd mind. *In* Lawrence—it's a town out on the Island—ah yes, Long Island. My younger sister, Linda, is finishing up her degree in Clinical Psych out at Stanford."

"Sounds lovely. And they all liked Robin?"

He frowned a bit. "No, actually Linda didn't and neither did Pete."

"Pete?"

"Pete Manaro, my best buddy. He's a homicide detective—works out of Midtown. Anyway, the three of us had dinner one night, Robin, Pete and me. I'd had a shit day and was out of sorts. There was a lot of tension in the air. Robin excused herself to go to the Ladies, and Pete turned to me and said, 'That's a helluva rod you've got up your ass.'"

Delia whooped. "Oh, I like Pete."

Daniel grinned. "Oh, yes—you two will definitely get along. Real *paesani*. Underneath the Quattrocento Raphael exterior, you're real peasant, Lady Delia. Comes out in the bedroom."

"Thank you," she said smiling. "And Raphael was Cinquecento. But no matter. So what was your response to your buddy?"

"I told him to fuck off, but Pete never lets up. He's like a dog gnawing a bone. Makes him a great cop, though. He said, 'Every time I see you with this bird, you're stiffer than a corpse's cock. Better give it some thought before you walk down the nave.' I did."

There was a long silence. Finally Delia said, *"Tunc?"* Daniel looked puzzled. "Then?"

"It was a nice life that Robin offered, two cars, two kids, a mortgage. My parents' version of the American Dream. The kind of person my parents and Robin saw me as and want me to be is not quite what I want. You see," he said with a shy grin, "I *don't* run to type."

"What *do* you want, Daniel?" Delia asked now, very intent.

He shook his head and stroked his hand along his chin in a gesture of thought that Delia now recognized and catalogued. "I don't really know. Not the world I've left, my parents' world, of that I'm sure. I've had tastes of things that have become important to me and enriched my life."

"Music," she said, and he nodded. "Poetry."

Again he gave her an affirmative reply. "But the lessons haven't been easy, and most of the learning has been done on my own. I want, I think, a wider horizon, a broader vision." Suddenly Daniel paused, and a flush rose to his face. "Do I sound like very much of a schmuck?" he asked.

"No, not very much," she said with a gentle smile.

"I met a lot of guys in college—Cornell—who took for granted those things I was just beginning to know about. I had a roommate freshman year, Martin Whitner—very mainline Philadelphia—

had gone to prep school and all that crap. He'd brought his stereo and record collection to school. Scriabin, Mussorgsky, Dave Brubeck, Cole Porter, Buxtehude . . . those names meant nothing to me. But I learned them. I wasn't raised on Telemann . . . I had to acquire an appreciation for his music on my own. And I have. But now I don't quite fit, you see, into a Brooks Brothers suit—nor do I fit in anymore with the Borscht Belt crowd."

"The what?"

"Never mind," Daniel said with a smile. Then his face grew serious again, and he said, "I know what I don't want. I'm not sure yet what I do want out of life. When I do know that, I'll let you know, Delia." The lovers' eyes met for a moment.

"Thank you," she said, suddenly realizing the sincerity of this last statement; it frightened her a little. "I would like to meet your buddy Pete. I want to pick his professional brain."

"Oh, yes, *do* tell me about your investigation so far."

"Well," Delia began, "the plot, as they say, thickens—actually it now sticks. When I spoke with Jason and Ned, they gave conflicting stories. Jason painted a future of marital bliss with Magda—house, *babbies,* antique shop. Said Magda had asked Ned for a divorce. Ned says absolutely not—that Jason was just another of Magda's fancy men."

"Who do you believe?"

"My inclination is to listen to Jason. I want to

believe that Magda had some idea of real happiness."

"But?"

"As much as I loathe Ned Hennessey — my instincts confirm what he claims."

"What does Charlotte say?"

"That she had hoped Magda was serious about Jason, but it had been too early to tell."

"Great," he said in some exasperation.

Delia paused for a long moment and studied Daniel Elliot's face. Once again, she took his hand. "Daniel, there's something else." He looked up inquiringly, and she went on, "I think I'm investigating more than Magda's drug use and abuse."

"More? . . . I don't get it, Delia."

"I think . . . ," she hesitated and then said, "I think this is actually a case of murder." Delia felt his body stiffen and his hand withdraw.

After a long moment Daniel said, "Listen, Delia. I'm a certified medical examiner, with a string of hot-shit degrees to my credit from a helluva lot of Ivy League schools — which puts me, professionally speaking, right up there in your class, your ladyship. You know, Cornell, Johns Hopkins, Columbia. Not Cambridge or Harvard perhaps, but it really does pass muster here as top-of-the-line learning. And I *examined* the body of Magdalene Maitland Hennessey and found *no signs of foul play.* None. That's my job and I do it very well. And I don't give a fuck about your feminine intuition. Maybe that kind of thing passes for knowledge in some circles, your ladyship, but not in mine."

Delia Ross-Merlani took a deep breath and counted to twenty—more than she had ever allowed anyone before. Then she looked hard at Daniel. "I'm not questioning your credentials or your skills. I have no doubt that they and you are top-drawer. But as you said, you looked at the body of Magdalene Maitland. You said that was *your* specialty. And her death, her murder, I think, has more to do with her mind—no, not mind, ψυχή—psyche, from the Greek. That word usually gets translated as mind or soul. It actually means 'breath'—the life source or life spirit. And that is what I believe someone murdered. This isn't 'feminine intuition.' It's some deep-seated sense that some grave injury was done to my friend. You said you admired my loyalty. Well, it extends even to this. I don't entirely understand it all yet. But I do credit and honor this feeling. And if I'm wrong, which I very well might be, and I make a total jackass of myself—then I'll accept those consequences. It's very little to risk, I think, out of love for my friend . . . two friends." She took his hand tentatively. "Please, will you help me?"

After what seemed like a long silence, Daniel's hand closed over hers. Delia shut her eyes for a moment and felt tears of relief flooding them: she hadn't quite realized how much had been riding on this moment until now. In a changed tone Daniel asked, "Where do you go from here?"

"I would like to do some research—talk to Magda's doctors."

"Okay."

"I would really appreciate meeting Detective Manaro, see if I can learn anything from him—techniques and all that."

Daniel smiled, and the last bit of tension between them finally dissolved. "I'm sure there's lots of techniques Pete would love to show you. But I'm not so sure how I feel about that—you two peasants might like each other too much."

Delia laughed, deep in the back of her throat. She got up and insinuated herself onto Daniel's lap, realizing again with pleasure how neatly she fit that space. "I've had more than my fill of pasta. Lately"—and she ran her hand through his thick hair—"my taste has run more to sampling pastrami, corned beef . . ." Her list remained unfinished as Daniel's mouth closed over her own.

Chapter Twelve

Advice From a Caterpillar

"The speed limit is thirty-five, Miss Delia, and traffic is rather stiff. I'm hurrying as much as humanly possible."

She frowned. "I know, *tesoro mio,* it's not your fault. So sorry about my grumbles." Delia was hastily completing her toilette in the back of the limousine. But really, it wasn't her fault. Daniel's call telling her to meet him in thirty minutes hadn't given her nearly enough time. Granted, she had perhaps dawdled over finishing *The Times* crossword, but really, she couldn't be rushed.

"The best Italian food in New York," Daniel had said. Well, Piazza La Fenice certainly didn't look like much, she thought, stepping out of the car. It reminded her of a leftover from a Fellini set from the fifties. Yet as she stepped inside, Delia was met by the familiar smells of garlic, wine and basil—and instantly felt that sense that she still knew to be dear. Then the imposing presence of the hostess.

"Yes?"

"Buona sera, Signora. Sono Signorina Ross-Merlani."

"Buona sera, Signorina. Sono Tina è benvenuto a Piazza La Fenice."

"Ah, ecco il mio amico," Delia said, giving Daniel a smile.

"Il dottore? Sì, sì," Tina said as she bustled over with Delia.

"Not bad, your ladyship—only thirty minutes late."

"But well worth the wait," said Daniel's companion.

"Ah, yes. Pete Manaro, Lady Delia Ross-Merlani."

"Tina, ascolta Lei? A Lady! *Una contessa inglese!"*

"Sì?"

Delia blushed and quickly gave a brief history of her lineage in Italian to Tina and Pete; she noticed Daniel's wicked smile at her obvious discomfiture. Finally, however, Tina seemed to forgive Delia her English mother, gave her a warm smile and accepted the young woman to her ample bosom. She brought a bottle of wine and said she would bring them *un pranzo spettacoloso.*

"Well, your ladyship, you're a lucky woman. Once Tina likes you, and that's rare, you're privy to some of the best food since *la mia nonna* died."

"Yet another notch . . ." Daniel murmured.

"Va te faire chier!" Delia hissed.

"What?" Pete said, looking at the lovers.

"Forget it," Delia said. "I'm glad to meet you, Pete. And please call me Delia." She again felt the appraising eye of Daniel's friend on her.

With a slight toss of her head, Delia turned her own gaze on her examiner. Joseph Peter Manaro was close on forty, dark-eyed, dark-haired, medium height, with a muscular, compact body. His mouth was hard, but there were promising full lips. She knew his kind at once—bright, tough, tender. *"Napolitano."*

He nodded, although she had asked no question. "Then the Bronx, now West 84th."

"Three addresses?" And she and Daniel started to laugh, sharing the same thought.

"Shit," Pete said, "I hate people who have just started fuckin'. They're so full of each other's juices and jokes."

Delia laughed. "Sorry—I do hate to run to type." Again she and Daniel exchanged charged looks.

"I know Danny-boy runs with a swell crowd, but wherever did he find you?"

"I have been friends with Charlotte and Magda Maitland since girlhood. Magda died in some unusual circumstances last month. Daniel did the post mortem, and I have asked for his help in my own investigation."

"Delia and Charlotte seem to believe that Magda was murdered," Daniel said, his voice empty of all inflection.

Delia flushed. "It might seem silly to some, but

we feel there are some loose threads; the only discernible pattern I can construct is that of someone having done away with Magda."

Pete drank down a glass of wine and turned to look at the woman before him. Then he put an olive in his mouth, chewed carefully on it, spit the pit into his hand and then swallowed. Taking another from the dish of rather extravagant antipasto that had miraculously appeared before them, he said, "Okay. What's the scoop?"

Delia briefly explained the details of Magda's illness and death. Pete listened critically, only interrupting here and there with a question or for clarification.

Finally he said, "Doesn't seem like much of a case—except for the colorful details. Your friend Magda sounds like a cliché of the murder victim in a dime novel—beautiful broad, blond, bright, promiscuous. Sorry to have missed her myself," he said with a tight grin. "Shot—yes. Neck broken—yes. That's how you get rid of that type. But I don't see a murder in your scenario."

Delia looked crestfallen and glanced at Daniel. His face was blank, wiped clean of comment. She let her fingers play with strands of her hair for a moment. Then, putting on a plucky smile she did not actually feel, she said, "So you don't think there's a case worth investigating?"

Pete Manaro turned his gaze full upon Delia, and she felt then the subtle strength in those eyes. "No. But *you* do. And that's the first thing a good detective has to go on." Delia began to speak, but he motioned her to silence. "If your nose tells you something smells fishy—then you have to follow the stink. Satisfy yourself. You may or may not have a case to investigate. But you do have questions worth answering. Do you have the time, money and means to carry on a thorough investigation?" Delia nodded. "Okay. What have you done so far?" Delia told him about her conversations with Jason and Ned. "What about your friend's will? Did she have life insurance?"

"I don't know," Delia said.

"Sex and money—major motives for crime. Check out both. Start by getting a thorough background on Magda's men—their money, women, expectations. Check out whoever else might have had a grudge against your friend. Or whoever else might have had a good reason to see her dead. Family, friends, everyone. Find out who might have benefited from her demise. You have three obvious 'suspects'—not a bad beginning."

"Three?"

"Husband, lover, sister."

"Charlotte? Charlotte? Oh, no! Charley adored Magda. And she's the most gentle person. Besides, she's the one who asked me to look into this."

Pete shrugged. "That might be her way of covering her own ass. Crying wolf throws suspicion on others—it's an old trick. Listen, the majority of murders in this town are committed within families. Sisters bump off sisters all the time. Maybe Charlotte needed her sister's money.

Maybe she had gambling debts. A guy. Maybe a kid. Maybe she was jealous of her sister's men. In love with her sister's husband. Lover. Who knows?"

For a moment the image of Charlotte and Jason came painfully to mind. Delia gave herself a quick pep talk on objectivity as she shook her head free of this image and listened once again to Pete.

"If you want to investigate, you can't give a shit about anyone involved in the case. *Who* you are has nothing to do with what you do." He smiled. "Think you can handle it?"

Delia did not answer at once. She stared for several long moments into the red depths of her wine. What did she want to do? Be with Charlotte? Near Daniel? Yes. Those were both clear. But why did she feel so strongly drawn to finding the answers to Magda's life and to her death?

Delia felt again that almost palpable connection she felt—had always felt—with Magdalene Maitland. They had been more than mere friends. They had crossed some unknown boundary together—lived some implicitly connected life. Although seeking each other rarely, there had always been an instant reawakening of their intimacy upon contact. Like a harmonic, Delia knew she had resonated to the dominant tones of Magda. They were attracted to, yet repelled by, the common chord each struck in the other. Both had always lived along a seemingly empty chasm and feared falling over the edge. In their relationship, there had been always this danger born of complicity.

Suddenly the walls of the restaurant blurred before Delia's eyes, and she saw once again Magda's face close to hers in one of those moments of intimate understanding they had shared. Magda's eyes had bored into her own, and the exquisite mouth had formed words that had become etched into Delia's heart, and been the frame of her life:

Wise wretch! with pleasures too refin'd to
   please;
With too much spirit to be e'er at
   ease;
With too much quickness ever to be
   taught;
With too much thinking to have
   common thought.
You purchase pain with all that joy
   can give,
And die of nothing but a rage to live.

Delia felt some terrible pull then on her heart, as if once again Magda's gaze was drawing her nearer and nearer that edge. She recognized that the search for diversion, challenge and fulfillment that had kept Magdalene Maitland hopelessly on the run also filled her own restless spirit. If only, Delia thought, she might find the answers in Magda's life and death before it was too late for herself.

When she looked up again, Pete Manaro seemed to be waiting patiently for a reply. Then she looked over at her Daniel, and saw his eyes searching her own, his lips poised on the edge of some implied inquiry. A flash ran through her then—*he knows!* It was as clear as if he had spoken aloud. A welter of confused feelings suddenly ran through Delia, most keenly a sense of respite and relief.

She looked back at Pete Mañaro. "I can handle it. Teach me; you'll find I'm a most receptive student."

Pete's mouth relaxed into a grin. "I'll bet you are." He looked hard at her again, but Delia felt only Daniel's searching gaze on her as Pete began his instructions on what he called "a dick's business."

When Delia awoke the next morning, the clock read 11:26. She turned lazily, feeling the lush lethargy that comes only from being in a lover's arms through the night. In the hollow left in Daniel's pillow, she found a manila envelope with her name on it. A note inside in Daniel's hand read: "Tools of your trade." Carefully unwrapping the tissue, she found an elegant wine-colored suede notebook and a delicate Cross pen. Etched on the barrel was the word, "Investigate."

Delia sat staring at the gift for a moment, her mind running almost automatically through this familiar analytical process. "Investigate . . . hmm . . . from the Latin *vestigatus,* I shouldn't wonder. Yes . . . *vestigare,* the past participle. *In* . . .

vestigare — to search into." And she recalled Daniel's look again — as if he could see and would know. Smiling at the beautiful gift, Delia commended Daniel for its appropriateness in both a literal and metaphorical sense.

Chapter Thirteen

Women and Children First

"The doctor will see you now."

As she shook Dr. Mathews's hand, murmuring "Professor Ross-Merlani," Delia was indeed acutely aware of throwing on her academic gown over her crisp Givenchy suit. Seating herself opposite the doctor, she began, "I was a close friend of the late Magda Maitland Hennessey and her sister Charlotte. On behalf of the family, I'm settling several things about Mrs. Hennessey's death."

"Sad business—such a lovely woman," Dr. Mathews said.

"Yes," Delia said, quickly sizing up the starchy, paternal psychiatrist. "Ms. Maitland—Mrs. Hennessey's younger sister—is terribly distressed over the death. She blames herself for failing to see the potential severity of Magda's situation. I thought perhaps I might be able to make some sense out of those last months and ease Ms. Maitland's mind."

"There was no way anyone could have foreseen the tragic seizure that killed Mrs. Hennessey. Sudden death often leaves a great deal of pain as its aftermath. Mightn't it be better if Ms. Maitland sought professional advice—to work out her feelings of grief and guilt?"

Delia smiled warmly, but with an inward sniff of distaste thought, *"Trou du cul."* Aloud, she said, "I agree that would be the best course. But I'm sure you understand that Ms. Maitland must seek help on her own initiative. At present, I think the best we can do is try to guide her to that awareness." Then she thought to herself, "Check mate," as the doctor sat back in his chair.

"Of course. How may I be of help?"

"Magda was having some problems these last years, both physiological and psychological. Was there any connection, do you think?"

"Well naturally, physical illness can lead to fear and apprehension. And unquestionably, Mrs. Hennessey had had a number of unfortunate problems . . . however . . ."

"Yes?" Delia said, making her face a study of rapt inquiry.

"Mrs. Hennessey's gastric complaints seemed to have no discernible cause. The mind can, I'm sure you know, wreak havoc on the body."

"I see, Doctor. What was *your* diagnosis?"

"Oh, depression, to be sure. She was often profoundly depressed, particularly prior to and during one of her attacks. I was called in by her internist a little more than a year ago because

Mrs. Hennessey appeared to be quite anxious, even hysterical at times."

"Her attacks were making her emotionally ill," Delia said, with just a hint of question in her voice.

Dr. Mathews, she saw, jumped eagerly at the proffered bait. "I'd say her emotional illness *caused* the attacks."

"Oh, how very dreadful," Delia said, her voice full of wonder as she gave her head a wistful shake. She remembered, however, reading in the hospital report of Magda's considerably elevated white cell count which this bastion of Vienna seemed clearly to have ignored. Something, something decidedly "medical," Delia knew, *had* been wrong with Magda.

"Have you any idea of the source of Mrs. Hennessey's problem? I believe it would be an enormous help to Charlotte in dealing with her own feelings. Perhaps it might spur her on to confer with you," Delia said, hating this but offering yet another carrot.

The doctor paused and placed his fingers tips to tips. "Well, I think Mrs. Hennessey and I had just about uncovered the source of her distress — several months ago, as a matter of fact — just before the hiatus in her analysis."

"Hiatus?"

"Yes," he said, shifting slightly in his seat. "Mrs. Hennessey had indicated that she wished to discontinue our sessions for a time while she uh . . . got her bearings, so to speak."

Delia kept her face absolutely impassive as she watched the doctor work his way through the treacheries of this admission. But she could not help but smile to herself as she remembered Charlotte's report of her sister's words when she had abruptly quit analysis. "Fuck this shit," had been Magda's characteristic verdict.

"And at that juncture, you had recognized Mrs. Hennessey's true difficulty?"

"Oh, yes," the analyst said slowly, "Mrs. Hennessey's attacks came on a fairly regular basis, you know. Almost monthly. These attacks often coincided with the *approach or onset of menses.*" Dr. Mathews leaned forward, his features reflecting his complete sense of rightful domain. "It's not an uncommon syndrome, I'm afraid. A great many women develop pain, anxiety, tension and depression prior to their menstrual period. As they recognize — albeit unconsciously — that they are about to menstruate, the fact of their not being pregnant, not fulfilling themselves as they must through a child, leaves them empty, bereft, and depressed. In Mrs. Hennessey's case, the premenstrual depression was extreme and precipitated physical attacks. When I asked her, Mrs. Hennessey described the pain as 'violent spasms,' 'agonizing contractions.' "

"Sounds like descriptions of labor," Delia brought out, ever the good student.

"Yes, but she indicated the pain was up near the region of her heart," he said. "Very tragic, really."

"Oh, yes," Delia murmured.

"I was particularly dismayed when Mrs. Hennessey left her husband last year. I had hoped she would stay with Professor Hennessey and that they could begin a family. I thought it would—as indeed it does for so many women—break the cycle of her unhappiness. I felt the pills," he concluded coolly, "were her undoing."

"Pills?"

"Why yes, the birth control pills she took. Many's the time I advised her to stop taking the pill and begin to accept her womanhood."

Delia ignored this last remark, which she considered fatuous in the extreme, as her mind raced ahead on this piece of information. She hadn't known that Magda was taking the pill. She made a mental note of this and snapped back to attention.

"You might want to take a look at some of the studies on 'Premenstrual Syndrome.' "

Delia got to her feet. "Oh, I certainly shall, Doctor. Thank you so much for your time. You *have* been an enormous help. I'll be sure to discuss all of this with Ms. Maitland," she added, relieved at last to be speaking some truth.

Outside Delia quickly found a phone booth, making another mental note to get a car phone. "Charley? Listen. One quick question. Was Mags on the pill? . . . For how long—do you know? . . . Right, I remember her abortion in San Francisco . . . oh, there were two abortions that year? . . . So after the second abortion, she went on the pill? That was about two years ago. Right? . . .

116

Okay—no, I haven't time to chat. I'll lunch with you tomorrow, say one-thirty at Olympe? *Bon! A bientôt.*"

Quickly, she dialed Daniel's number and impatiently tapped her foot till she was put through. *"Mia cara,* would birth control pills show up in a post mortem?"

"Of course—why? And where are you?"

"Fifth Avenue and Seventy-second. Listen— Magda was taking birth control pills."

"Are you sure?" Daniel asked slowly.

"Yes, according to her shrink, who by the way reaches new heights of misogynous *merde.* And Charley confirms, about the pills, that is."

"Not good enough. Check with her gynecologist, pharmacist and Jason. We have to be *certain,* Delia. If that's so, this would be the first really concrete discrepancy. You might just have a case."

Delia felt her face flush with pleasure. *"Ay, Santa Maria,* it will be worth the seeming hours of Dr. Mathews's drivel just for that *bon mot* of info. You would not believe *his* theory of Magda's problem!"

"Tell me tonight. I'll make you dinner—you can provide the entertainment."

"I'd prefer to be a duet."

He laughed. "That, too. At seven. Sharp! Delia, not sevenish!"

"Ah, it's starting, Dr. Elliot."

"What?"

"Your trying to change me. Make me into what you want me to be." And then there was a charged silence between them. Although their tones had been bantering, each recognized that they had innocently stumbled upon and hit an exposed nerve in the other.

"Sorry. I'll . . . hold the soufflé until you arrive."

"Seven," Delia said, "with bells on and a bottle of Tocai '78 to go with the meal. *Ciao*." Delia quietly replaced the receiver; her hand, she noticed, was trembling just a bit.

Delia sat down in the back of the car, instantly grateful for the coolness of its interior. As Mr. MacPhee pulled out into traffic, her mind suddenly focused on a scene from her life just as a film image comes up sharply on a screen. Pregnant, some years before in Paris while she had been frantically working on her dissertation, Delia had sent an SOS to her friend's sister. Charley would have come, she knew, but somehow Delia sensed Magda would better understand the feelings of anger and betrayal she had felt. Magda had, of course, known a doctor. He was gruff and unpleasant, but he had done a good enough job, she supposed. He had given Delia a local, which didn't help much, but the intense pain had only lasted for several minutes.

No, it was mostly the dreadful waves of bleeding that had disturbed her. Hours and hours of it. Magda had stayed with her, joking with her, distracting her, cheering her along. They had talked of so many things during that long night. And now suddenly Delia could feel once again Magda's

118

hand as it had gently smoothed back Delia's hair from her sweaty brow. She recalled how in the lulls of conversation, Magda had recited verse after verse from *The Faerie Queene* as if this somehow might counteract the pain and fear that Delia felt.

Yet the very next night, Delia had felt so much better that they had gone to the see the American Ballet Theatre and delighted in the *grand jetés* and calves of Richard Bustamante. Afterward, they had gone for a long walk, and found themselves at last standing on a bridge. Magda had begun at once as if on cue to recite from Edmund Spenser,

> " 'And painful pleasure turns to
> pleasing pain.' "

Then with a grand gesture, Delia had thrown her diaphragm into the Seine. Laughing, they had returned to the hotel, drunk icy champagne and fallen asleep in each other's arms. As soon as Delia had finished her work, she had returned to London and gotten a prescription for birth control pills.

"So Magda followed that route, too, it seems," she thought, "the pain . . . the pill . . . the pleasure." Delia felt this wide smile suddenly fill her as she realized how engaged she had become in this work. Nothing she had ever done before, she knew, had quite captured the fullness of her intent as this investigation.

And then Delia got out her notebook and began

to make clear and precise notes on the morning's conversation. She did this knowing it was correct procedure. But she also wanted to put the more worrisome words of Daniel Elliot from her mind.

Chapter Fourteen

A Musical Interlude

Daniel opened the door, took the wine from her hand, planted his cool lips on hers, then handed Delia the score for Book One of *The Well-Tempered Clavier*. "Sing for your supper, toots," he said.

Delia's puzzled look melted into one of shock, astonishment and then joy at the sight of his living room. Several bookcases had been removed and the couch pushed against the wall to accommodate a Neupert Harpsichord. She walked slowly to it, opened it and played several arpeggios. Delia turned to Daniel, her eyes hastily blinking back the tears. She put her arms round him, hugging him closely to her.

"Rented for the occasional," he said. "When you're here, I can hear. Selfish actually, I so rarely get to concerts; something always seems to come up."

Delia began to shake with laughter, her body tight against his.

"I know it's not the finest of instruments, but there's slim pickings in harpsichord rentals. Well, let's get to work—you Bach the notes, I'll beat the yolks." He kissed the top of her head, and she groaned; they both felt rescued from the intense emotion his gift and words had aroused in them.

Delia spent some time carefully tuning the instrument; a visceral pleasure flooded her as she did this. Then she sat down and played several Bach preludes as well as the Telemann they had listened to their first night together. How much she loved this music, she thought, and was lost in her own performance when Daniel quietly announced, "Dinner is served, your ladyship."

Over soufflé, salad and wine, Delia gave a summary of the rest of her day. "I checked with Magda's gynecologist. He gave her a prescription for a year's worth of Ortho Novum on January 6, 1990. According to her pharmacy, she refilled the prescription this January."

"Did you check with Jason?"

"Not yet—I left word with his answering service to call me. He's out tonight with Charley seeing the new Met production of *Don Giovanni*."

Daniel looked up at her. "Are they an item?"

"I don't know. I don't think so. Probably they're just filling a need for each other, hanging on to memories of Magda."

"They're both so young," Daniel said.

"Actually, Charley is older than I am," Delia said.

"I know, but she seems scarcely older than Jason. Have there been any men in her life?"

"Oh, a few, but nothing serious. It will take a very special man to appreciate Charlotte Maitland. And get through her defenses."

"What's that sweet child got to be defensive about?" Daniel asked.

"We all have something, Daniel. All of us are hiding from some place." She paused, but he allowed this loaded statement to pass unquestioned at least for now.

"Both Maitland girls were deeply wounded by their parents' deaths, Magda even more than Charlotte. I think it's what makes Charley childlike, sometimes fearful. She's afraid of losing love, so she doesn't seek it."

"And Magda?"

"Oh, Magda was gobbling up experiences in order not to face her own loneliness." Delia heard her voice suddenly trembling a bit, and she sensed her lover's eyes now hard upon her. She went on brightly, "That, however, was *not* her analyst's view."

"Oh, and what did he think?" Daniel asked, producing a Miss Grimble's marble cheese cake and Perrier-Jouët for dessert.

"Think? His type never *thinks*. The good Dr. Mathews said Magda's monthly curse was due to her cursed monthlies — to coin a phrase cum Daniel Elliot. That her gastric attacks were a kind of premenstrual crampies taken to the extreme. Magda was unhappy because she was not having a baby. That, he said, made her believe that her tummy ached. How easy for *lourdaux* like him to dismiss any woman's problem as a 'woman's problem.' "

"Shades of Karen Horney," Daniel murmured.

"Oh, yes indeed. I glanced through Dr. Karen Horney's stuff today on Dr. Mathews's advice, don'tcha know. A psychiatrist most aptly named, I'm sure, if her theories are any indication."

Daniel smiled and then said, "Still the birth control pills are an intriguing bit of data. Although it doesn't add up to much. She may have been prescribed the pills but not taking them at the time of her death."

"Jason will let us know that. I simply must find a way of asking him without letting him see the significance of the question."

Daniel smiled again. "Very good. I'll be sure to tell Professor Pete that you're becoming a real detective. He'll like that. He liked *you,* by the way. Said he appreciated a broad that could talk blue in so many colorful languages."

Delia returned his grin. "Pete Manaro, I should imagine, likes almost any nicely filled skirt that comes his way. He looks at women as meat on a rack."

Daniel laughed and nodded. "I'll tell him that— he'll be quite pleased."

Delia reached out her hand, unbuttoned Daniel's shirt and began to stroke his smooth chest. "I say, Doctor, speaking of . . . care to try a little tenderloin?" she whispered, her lips seeking him out, sure now that she would find him.

Chapter Fifteen

Little Boys Blue

Delia nervously played with the strands of her chignon, caught herself in the act and smiled self-consciously as she could almost see Mrs. Mac's disapproving glance. Then she tucked the hair in, firmly repositioned her hair pins, and put her hat back on. It was hot for May; even the plashing of the Paley Park fountain did not make her feel any cooler. When she saw Jason Howland approaching, however, Delia brought her face back into a mask of self-possession.

"Hello. How was the . . . shoot? . . . right . . . the shoot?"

"Yes . . . shoot. Dull. A lot of crotch shots—an ad for jeans. But it pays the rent."

Delia nodded knowingly, though she had never written out a rent check, or a check for anything else, in her life. "Don't you like modeling at all?" Delia asked, her face now full of the tenderest inquiry.

Jason shook his head vehemently, and once more

Delia was reminded of a puppy's muzzle. "No, it's a shit job."

"How about 'treading the boards'? Do you enjoy that?"

"Sometimes—depends on the part. But mostly not."

"Why don't you try something else," Delia suggested.

Jason's beautiful features flushed dark. "I had planned to, you see . . . with Magda."

"Oh, I'm so sorry, I didn't mean to rake up your pain," Delia brought out in a rush as she mentally gave herself a pat on the back for this last maneuver.

"Oh, that's okay, Delia. I'm really glad you suggested we meet. I feel the need to talk about Magda still, and I know I can talk to you about her. And to Charley."

Delia gave an imperceptible flinch; this familiar "Charley" jarred in her ears. Filing this away for the moment she went on, "I spoke with Magda's psychiatrist. Charlotte has, you know, asked me to rather sort things out for her. I found Dr. Mathews to be a dreadful specimen."

Jason chuckled. "Magda called him *le crapaud châtre*—the castrated toad."

Delia gave a deep-throated laugh. She *would* indeed miss Magdalene. "He very neatly talked round Magda's decision to quit analysis."

"Oh, I'll bet. Magda said he was pissed as hell."

"Why did she stop, Jason?"

"Mathews told Magda she was 'afraid of her own womanhood.' Can you believe it—Magda!? He kept urging her to go back to Ned."

"Why?"

Jason shrugged. "He said her pain would stop if she became pregnant."

"Sounds a bit odd, that."

"Magda thought it was total bullshit. And of course"—here he grinned, and Delia's heart opened once again to him—"she told that to the toad in just so many words."

"But didn't she want to have children? I thought you had said . . ."

"Oh, yes, someday we planned a family," Jason explained, his face looking very manly all of a sudden. "But not until we'd really settled down."

"Yes—well, I always say we must be thankful for all those loopy things!"

" 'Loopy things'?"

"Oh, yes . . . whatever they're called. The IUD. Magda had one put in after the first—" Suddenly Delia clapped her hand over her mouth. "Oh, *merde!* When shall I ever learn to be more careful. I . . . I . . . ," she murmured in some confusion.

Jason reached out and took Delia's hand. "It's all right, Delia. I knew about the abortions. Magda and I had no secrets from each other."

Delia gave his hand a little comforting squeeze. This, however, gave her a moment to reflect that for a woman who prided herself on duplicity, Magdalene Maitland certainly seemed to have con-

128

vinced her men that she was completely honest with each of them. Delia doffed her hat to her late friend.

Jason let go of Delia's hand. He seemed to stare out at the water rushing along the wall before he said, "But you're wrong about the IUD, Delia. It was removed before the second abortion. After that Magda went on the pill."

"Oh." Delia nodded. "A smart move. Those pills do give one such a sense of control."

"Hmmm," Jason murmured, "yes, I suppose so. And I think that was something my Magda wanted and needed."

"Yes," Delia said, surreptitiously consulting her pocket watch which she inherited from her maternal great-grandmother. She dearly hoped Mrs. Mac had set it to the correct time before slipping it into the pocket of her Perry Ellis skirt. "I hear you and Charlotte have been stepping out."

He nodded. "She's very sweet, and I really care about her."

Delia beamed. "She's very dear. Let's all have dinner. River Cafe—say day after tomorrow?"

"Sounds great. I don't want to lose touch with either of you. You're kind of like family to me."

Jason's eyes had filled with tears, and rather unexpectedly Delia felt herself truly touched to the quick. In spite of her doubts about Magda's death, her fears for Charlotte, the investigation, she felt herself increasingly drawn to the ingenuousness of this young man. For a second, she envied Magda having had his devotion.

"Of course, Jason. We *are* a family. Ah, I've got to run; I'm late as usual. Fix up the dinner details with Charley." Delia gave the young man a warm embrace and hastened to her waiting car. She dialed Daniel's number on her newly installed telephone. As she listened to the rings at the other end, she jotted down several facts in her notebook.

"Listen, my dear. I'm having dinner at Charley's *ce soir.* Get in touch with Detective Pete and join us for coffee. I think we should all have a talk. Tell him this Merlani angler finds the fishy smell is becoming a downright stench."

"I'll cab it back to the hotel later, *tesoro mio,*" Delia said as Mr. MacPhee helped her from the car.

"To the hotel—tonight?"

"Well, perhaps not. I'll ring you and the missus when I know my plans."

"Be careful, Miss Delia," Mr. MacPhee said with uncharacteristic emphasis.

"You mean of lurking men?"

"Not just lurking, Miss Delia," he said pointedly. "Look carefully where you're stepping along just now. *Best to take something to avizandum, my douce lassie.*"

Delia gazed up fondly at Mr. Gregory MacPhee. He rarely lapsed into dialect and then only when he had something special to say to her. He was worried, she could see, worried about her and Daniel.

"Dinna fash yerself, I'll be canny," she said and was glad to see her Scots elicit a smile. She gave his forehead a quick kiss, and then like the little girl she had been and he had nurtured, she gave a brief wave and watched him drive off.

Wasn't Mr. MacPhee looking just a bit peaked lately? she wondered. She must arrange a holiday for the darling Macs soon. Perhaps home to the Isle of Skye, she decided, although sans their mistress.

As she approached Charlotte's building, Delia saw, as one perceives a signature on the edge of a huge canvas, a flash of red beard as a figure ducked into a doorway across the street. She paused, thought for a moment, and then continued on her way.

Delia pretended to wait for the elevator, when in truth, it was standing right in front of her. She took out her compact, fussed a bit with her hat and, in doing so, trained the glass on that particular doorway across the street. After several long moments, Delia felt her efforts were amply rewarded by the sight of a tall red-bearded man emerging from the shadows. Delia snapped her compact shut and got into the elevator. Oh, it was certainly a pity that no passerby was there. One might have witnessed an incandescent smile light up and transform to beauty the face of Viscountess Ross-Merlani as the elevator ascended to the eleventh floor.

Chapter Sixteen

Rhyme and Reason

"What are you going to do with all of it?" Delia began as her glance fell on the stack of cartons piled in a corner.

"I don't know, actually. It took me ever so long to go through Magda's things and crate them. I haven't really had a chance to consider what I'll do now. I'll keep the jewelry, of course—send the clothing to jumble, I guess. Aside from that, there's mostly her books."

Delia nodded. "Add those to your library."

Charlotte shook her head. "Some, I guess. You should take a look at them, Delia. They're more in your line—mostly poetry."

"Not art?"

"No. Ned kept those. These poetry books were with Jason. And, oh, Magda's keys weren't in Jason's flat. But I did find her wedding band.

I've put it in the vault with her other jewels."

"Did you tell Ned?"

"Why, no," Charlotte said, looking up in surprise. "Should I?"

"No. Tell Ned nothing. Or Jason or anyone for that matter. As far as anything concerning Magda goes, this is a good time to display some of our British 'stiff upper lip' and 'clam up,' if you'll pardon the American mixed metaphor."

"Whom and exactly what do you suspect, Delia?" Charlotte asked.

"At this point, I suspect everyone, Charley, including you."

"Including me? Oh la! I'm so glad. I think I make an admirable suspect."

"Do you? Pete Manaro, whom you'll meet this evening, thinks so, too."

"Oh, really? How very exciting," Charlotte said, and her eyes lit up in apparent delight. Delia thought Charlotte looked especially lovely at this moment, and the two friends exchanged smiles that connoted absolute trust.

When Charlotte repaired to the kitchen to see to hors d'oeuvres, Delia strolled over to the pile of cartons and pulled out a volume. "There's quite a number here. Hmmm, *The Victorian Poets*. Well, Mags certainly loved a good verse." Delia opened the book and saw the inscription on the flyleaf in Magda's tiny exquisite hand: "To my darlingest Jason, I love you. Magdalene." Delia noted with surprise that Jason had parted with this lover's gift. But, she finally concluded, like taste there was no accounting for grief. Delia continued flipping through the book, noticing many more notes in her late friend's writing.

"Yes," Charlotte said, coming in from the kitchen, "she adored poetry. There was something *fine* in my sister."

"Yes, there was."

At the peal of the bell, Charlotte turned to answer the door. With only half an ear, Delia listened to Daniel's and Pete's greetings as she glanced down at the volume now on top of the stack, *The Romantic Poets*. She felt a dog-eared page and turned to it, murmuring aloud its marked lines:

> " 'They name thee before
>   me,
> A knell to mine ear;
> A shudder come o'er me—
> Why wert thou so dear?
> They know not I knew
>   thee
> Who knew thee too well:
> Long, long shall I rue
>   thee
> Too deeply to tell.' "

Suddenly self-conscious, Delia glanced up, her

eyes meeting Daniel Elliot's. She realized he had undoubtedly caught the last lines, and she saw that his face looked pale from a strongly suppressed emotion.

"Researching?" he asked, his voice hard.

"Investigating," Delia replied, snapping the volume shut. "One of Magda's."

"Thinking of taking a leaf from her book?"

Delia gave a shake of her head and began to reply when Pete's voice cut in. "Can't you two fight and fuck on your own time?"

"It amazes me, Manaro, how you always have the correct sentiment for every occasion," Daniel commented dryly.

"I used to write goddam Hallmark cards," Pete rejoined. Suddenly he turned to Charlotte. "I'm truly sorry, Miss Maitland, please forgive my rough language. I think Her Royal Highness brings out the worst in me."

"I believe," Charlotte said in an engaging tone which Delia had never heard from her friend, "that Delia should be called her ladyship. I prefer to be called Charlotte. As far as your language is concerned, no apologies please. I've heard it all before, and I assure you, it's perfectly acceptable to me. I value honesty more than courtesy, Detective Manaro."

Delia, tremendously taken aback by this little speech, was now completely nonplussed by the smile exchanged between the detective and her friend.

"Kind of like watching a non-animated version of *Beauty and the Beast,* wouldn't you say,' " Daniel said, his voice *sotto voce* in her ear. Unable to help herself, Delia began to giggle; she suddenly recognized with joy that she was certainly falling in love with this charming, obstinate, complex man.

"Coffee and Benedictine?" Charlotte suggested as everyone settled into seats.

"No booze for me—I'm still on duty," Pete grumbled.

"Nor me either—I've still my duty to do," Daniel said eyeing Delia, who, much to her chagrin, started to giggle again.

When everyone was seated with appropriate beverages, Delia drew out her notebook. An expectant silence fell over the other three. Aware of all eyes upon her, she forced herself to speak in a firm voice.

"I started out with a vague disquiet, several things that did not add up and one piece of data that seemed contradictory. To that I can now add a piece of hard evidence."

Pete looked up questioningly, but Delia went on, "Let me back up somewhat and present it to you in its entirety. First, both Charlotte and I felt that there was something wrong in the account of Magda's death. Charlotte knew for certain that Magda had stopped using any drugs, yet Daniel found some sedatives in her bloodstream. Our sense of something wrong began with that discrepancy.

"Now for the things that don't add up: One, Magda had a long history of gastric problems which upon autopsy appeared unfounded. Two, Jason Howland says Magda had asked her husband for a divorce. Ned denies this. Someone is lying.

"Now for the contradiction: The autopsy showed small traces of secobarbital sodium, yet Magda claimed she had stopped using drugs. We have been unable to account for how this drug got into her system." Pete opened his mouth, but again Delia went on. "I checked with Magda's internist, gynecologist, psychiatrist and the Pathmark Pharmacy that filled all her prescriptions. None of the doctors issued a prescription to Magda for Seconal in any form." Delia paused and said, "Nor have any prescriptions for Seconal been filled for Ned Hennessey or Jason Howland within the last year."

"How do you know that?" Pete asked.

"I went to"—and here she consulted her notes—"thirty-eight pharmacies in the neighborhoods where Ned lives and works. Posing as Mrs. Hennessey, I explained"—her voice took on a disarming lost little girl tone—" 'I've mislaid the bottle of dear Neddy's pills and can't recall the date of the prescription. And oh, my husband will be so angry if I don't get them—and won't Mr. So-and-So be a dearie and help?' "

"Nice going," Pete said.

"You have been a busy little peeress," Daniel said approvingly.

"How do you know about Jason?" Charlotte asked.

"Oh! Mrs. MacPhee, in her saddest Scots burr, went to twenty-six drug stores near Jason and asked for the same help for 'her wee laddie.' So going on the assumption that neither man had a reason to hide a prescription for Seconal, we can assume that neither had the pills in his possession. Hence, Magda did not get them from either of her men."

"That's terrific," Daniel said.

"There's always the streets," Pete countered.

"No, not Magda. She wouldn't buy drugs on the streets," Delia said. "Too risky."

"No," Charlotte said firmly, "Magda always got her drugs from either her friends or by convincing a doctor that she had a bona fide complaint. She never got her drugs from a . . . a dealer. Besides, she wouldn't have had to in this case. Dr. Mathews wanted to give her a sedative, and she absolutely refused. She was not going to take any more drugs. Why, then, would she get the drugs illicitly?"

"Right, I'll buy that," Pete said. "Okay, Delia, your contradiction holds water. What's the hard evidence?"

Delia looked at Daniel, and quietly he said, "In the autopsy I did find traces of Seconal in her body, but that's all. Yet, by her own admission and according to her doctors, pharmacy, lover, and sister, Magda Maitland Hennessey was taking birth control pills."

Pete sat up. "Are you sure?"

"Oh, yeah. Considering Magda's drug history, age and sudden death, we did every test in the book: drug and toxicology screens, scans, radioimmunoassay—you name it. Birth control pills produce metabolites that we can discern from the natural hormones produced by the body. We found none of these. All we found were traces of barbiturates."

Pete sipped at his coffee and then said, "So you think someone slipped her reds instead of the pill?"

"Yes," Delia and Charlotte said at the same moment.

"But why? There wasn't enough to kill her. Right?"

Daniel shook his head.

"But," Delia said suddenly, "it made her *calm*. Right, Charley? You said Mags was really happy and at ease these last months." Charlotte nodded. "Perhaps the killer needed to keep Magda off guard—relaxed." She paused and then said as the idea solidified in her mind, "Or pregnant."

"But," Daniel said softly, "that still doesn't give us proof of murder or . . . even a means."

Delia sat back in her chair, knowing she had played her best hand and still not made enough tricks to make the contract.

Pete stood up, brushing imaginary crumbs from his faded jeans. He looked down at Delia. "Hey, *donna!* You did good work. Fine work. Someone went to a lot of trouble to give your friend a drug she wouldn't take. Your original 'contradiction' paid off. That's good—the mark of a born detective. But you've just begun. Now keep at it. Bring me a means of death and we'll get ourselves a murderer."

"Then, you think it *was* murder?" Charlotte asked, her voice now a mixture of anxiety, relief and excitement.

"No. But I'm sure nuts about the idea of you guys trying to turn it into one. A real treat. Well, if you'll excuse me, I have to question a man who stabbed his wife and stepson because there was no cream for his coffee this morning."

"How mundane," Delia said.

Pete shrugged. "It's a living," and the two exchanged a smile.

"I'll see you to the door," Charlotte said, bounding up.

"Et maintenant?" Delia said.

"Maintenant, we go back to my place, make love half a dozen times, sleep a bit and see the new day in wrapped in each other's extremities."

"Sounds grand," Delia said. "Then what?"

"Then you'll think it through all over again and begin the next leg of your investigation."

"What do *you* think, Daniel?"

He paused, and then quite suddenly his expression changed. Very softly he said, *"I think I love you, Delia."*

Charlotte came dashing back into the room, beginning in mid-sentence, ". . . Oh, Delia, it's really working out, isn't it? Isn't it?"

"Yes," Delia said steadily as she met Daniel's searching gaze. "Yes, it really is working out, Charley."

Chapter Seventeen

The Family Way

Lady Delia Ross-Merlani stared up at a Flemish tapestry in the Medieval Gallery of the Metropolitan Museum of Art. She had been at this post in silence most of this afternoon and the previous day. Something about the delicate, disdainful face of the figure, entitled *Lady With a Falcon,* reminded Delia of her lost friend.

Completely unaware of the look of wary concern on the face of the guard, Delia's eye took in once again the elaborately embroidered flowers and trees set against a red rich background. Then she focused her gaze on the white rabbits scattered throughout the work.

Delia frowned. Who, she thought, would have wanted Magda Hennessey pregnant? And why? Both Ned and Jason had at one time or another access to her birth control pills. One of them must have made the switch. Why Seconal? she wondered. To keep Magda calm, dreamy. Surely less peripatetic. Perhaps in that case more amorous? Did that fit?

But who would have gained if Magda indeed became pregnant? Ned? But only if it were his child and Magda had kept it. Considering her track record in that department, the odds weren't good, Delia knew. Perhaps Dr. Mathews had shared his crackpot theories with Ned. Magda has a baby and stays with the daddy. Could this have been Ned's thinking? Delia gave a little involuntary shudder.

Jason? Could he have thought of the same thing? Feared he might lose Magda and their dream future? Could he have tried to tie Magda to him by a child? Oh, that seemed crazy to Delia. Jason was scarcely more than a child himself.

Delia had checked out the birth control pills Magda was prescribed. The little white pills were quite different from Seconal's red capsules. Whoever had made the substitution must have arranged to have sedatives prepared that looked like Magda's prescription for Ortho Novum. "Designer drugs." Yes, Delia remembered hearing discussions of such things in the dressing rooms and after hours clubs and gyms, when she had been with the ballet. All right. That's what she needed to find out next. By whom — and for whom — was this custom-made drug prepared.

Delia Ross-Merlani got quietly to her feet. She walked slowly through the length of the galleries, twirling her finger through wisps of her hair. "It's time to go back," she could feel herself explaining to Magda. "I guess I need to go back to that world, Mags. We parted company, you and I, pretty much at the door, didn't we? You went on in and I went on ahead. But I guess I have to go back now. Follow this lead. Follow the trail. Pick up one of those strands of my own life that I've let so long dangle."

When she reached the car, Delia slid silently into the backseat. In almost the same smooth movement, she picked up her car phone and dialed for assistance.

As she ascended the stairs, Delia gave in to a little wave of anxiety. Perhaps she would have been better off with the new Repetto shoes or Capezio's Aerial—everyone seemed to be trying those nowadays. But oh, she'd worn Pavlowas since her earliest days on *pointe* at the Royal Ballet School . . . and besides. . . .

Delia frowned for a moment at her own silliness—then laughed. It was what all dancers did when they had a case of nerves—discussed toe shoes in all their variations, as if a change of shank might settle every question and stomach. But then, almost before she realized it, Delia found herself in front of the studio of Isabel Larsen. She hesitated just a moment more before putting her finger to the bell.

How had it all begun, she wondered, this epoch in her life? With Papa's arriving unexpectedly in Paris that time. Yes, his and Adela's paths had crossed — swords as well, Delia supposed. And then he had come by late one day to fetch her from Lady Ross's apartments at the Ritz — more, Delia realized now, to assert some sovereignty over his wife than actually because he had wanted to spend time with his daughter. *"Dove desidere andare, Giulietta?"* he had asked her, speaking to her in his offhand way, in his native tongue, addressing her always by the name that had been his mother's.

Where did she want to go? Delia had asked herself at age seven. How to tell him the truth? *I want to go home, Papa. I want to go home to Rosemuir and live with you and with Adela, and every day we shall have marmalade tart for dessert.* But already wise in the way of the world of her parents, Delia had simply shrugged — that gesture born and bred into her thin shoulders through the lines of Merlani fishermen.

How he had decided to take her to the ballet Delia had never actually discovered. But the next thing she could recall was sitting in a box at the Paris Opera House and seeing a vision that would be seared into her consciousness for the rest of her life: Isabel Larsen dancing Odette, the Swan Queen.

She had long been a legend even then — the cool, contained *prima ballerina assoluta* from

Sweden whose movements could suddenly soar with fire, her body arching to greater and greater grace, taking her audience along with her in this seemingly endless quest. Delia had, of course, been to the ballet before: indifferent *Nutcrackers,* uninspiring *Giselles* on countless occasions in which Lady Ross had required the presence of her daughter. But none of those performances had ever been more than mere show to Delia until the moment in Act Two of *Swan Lake* when Isabel Larsen executed a series of travelling *fouettés* and then *entrechats* and *relevés* at such tremendous speed that the seven-year-old Delia quite literally leapt from her seat in joy. And at that moment, the child had felt a shift deep inside her being—something she would only know again when she first encountered the text of the twelfth century poet Bernard de Ventadour; first heard a recording of Wanda Landowska performing Bach, first felt Daniel Elliot's cool lips on her own—moments that she knew deepest within her self that sense of belonging, of home.

Delia had seen the great Isabel Larsen dance many times after that and, like most of the other girls in the ballet school, had wept at the news reports of the ballerina's unexpected decision to retire from the stage at the age of thirty-three. Delia remembered still the photographs of the beautiful woman's face splashed across headlines nearly twenty years before. Vividly, she could still picture the huge eyes jumping out at her off the page as her own had filled with tears.

Now at the sound of the bell, Delia found those eyes suddenly gazing out from the open doorway at her. With only the briefest of nods, she was directed to follow Isabel Larsen into the studio. Delia extended her hand, and the older woman lightly returned her grasp. "I appreciate your seeing me, Madame."

In the bright daylight of the studio, Isabel Larsen turned her gaze full upon the other woman's face and form. "And what might I do for you, Lady Ross-Merlani?" Delia started a bit at the sound of her title; when she had telephoned and asked for an appointment, she had merely given her name. "Ah, I do remember who you are. I recall seeing you at the school in your early years. You were too thin even then I recall, but I agreed with Sir Frederick that you would fill out and be quite fine. Ah yes, I know well who you are, Lady Ross-Merlani."

Delia looked round for a moment at the studio—feeling the familiar give of the special flooring, seeing herself reflected over and over in the mirrors on all walls. "Then, I am not merely appreciative, Madame, but deeply honored as well."

Isabel Larsen looked at the other woman once more, and Delia felt the intensity of that appraisal. "And once again I ask, what might I do for you, Lady Ross-Merlani?"

Delia took a deep breath. "I would like to arrange to take class with you. I have not danced for a number of years and would like now to resume my training."

Isabel Larsen's face remained impassive, but there was an undercurrent to her voice. "You wish to train once more to dance professionally—to return to the stage?"

Delia glanced down for a moment. Slowly, she shook her head. "No. I do not wish to dance professionally again. This training would be something for myself only. I would like to return to taking company class again—but I am not quite up to snuff, as they say. As I will be in New York for some time, I thought I would take the opportunity to study with you, Madame."

Although Delia had, in fact, prepared this little speech, she could hear how thin it might sound to someone else. But she could not exactly confide her very mixed motives for returning to the ballet world to Isabel Larsen. She could not explain that in order to find her way back to that world of the demimonde in which a "designer drug" could be easily—one could say almost routinely—obtained, she had to return to the world of dancers and artists that peopled the undercurrent of any big city's cultural life. That world full of broken hearts and broken dreams from which she had fled some years before. She could not explain to Isabel Larsen how pulled she felt by that world still and how frightened

148

she felt by it. Magda had been lost in that world; of that, Delia was certain. And in pursuit of her friend's killer she must go back and learn to navigate once more through its trickiest waters. Recognizing this, Delia had decided to arm herself before entering into that life again. She could not simply return to a ballet company class until she knew that once more her body was at its veritable peak of performance. She must, in that world of deceit, be able to rely absolutely on her own integrity.

Delia watched as Isabel Larsen walked across the studio. Even now, she could see the extraordinary verve in the very slightest gestures of the other woman, and Delia felt herself in the presence of something larger than even the life she had known. Without turning back to face Delia, Isabel went on, "You had risen to soloist at the Royal. But your performance was erratic. You often dashed off to . . ."—and here she waved one of her elegant hands to denote the world at large—"pursuing as it were, other things. Then you danced with the Monte Carlo and were offered principal roles. I recall one performance I saw in Rome of *Pas de Quatre* and the notices you received. 'A new star is shimmering on the dance horizon.' But suddenly you went . . . where?"

"Cambridge," Delia said softly. "Queens College, Cambridge."

"To?"

"To complete my doctoral work in Medieval Studies."

"And then you taught for some time?"

"Yes," Delia said, feeling the full weight of this interrogation.

"And weren't there also some kind of music performances as well?"

"Yes," Delia replied. "I play the harpsichord and was frequently a guest artist with the Waverly Consort and the London Baroque Philharmonia."

"And you also married . . ."

Suddenly Delia felt her back stiffen. "Yes, Madame! I married and taught at Harvard and competed as an equestrian in the 1984 Olympics and traveled a good deal and did many, many—too many—things. Yes, I have done a great many things, Madame. And now I wish to dance once again." Delia could feel now the waves of disapprobation emanating from the older woman opposite her.

When Isabel Larsen spoke she did nothing to disguise this note in her voice. "There are so many young men and women who come to see me, Lady Ross-Merlani. Many who come from halfway round the globe to study with Isabel Larsen. They are willing to give up much—to have this, this one thing only. They want to dance! They feel it in every part of themselves— this drive, this desire. I have little energy and time, Lady Ross-Merlani, and too many calls upon it. I do not know that I wish to waste it with a woman who does 'many, many too many things.' I train *dancers*." And with that, Isabel Larsen turned away—her whole body a gesture of dismissal.

Once more, Delia felt that sense of how she must look in another's eyes—and she knew that this woman's understanding of her was as damning and as hollow as Daniel Elliot's had initially been. After a long pause Delia said, "I always believed, Madame, that a dancer is something one *is*. Not something one does. If I never rise up on *pointe* again, if I never begin that lift that becomes a leap, I will still *be* a dancer. A dancer is what I am, Madame."

Delia watched as her words sunk into the retreating back of Isabel Larsen . . . the dancer who for her generation and the generations to follow would always epitomize that word. And Delia knew then that something more was at stake here than merely taking ballet classes again. That in winning this woman's confidence she might begin to trust in her own.

Isabel Larsen turned back and looked hard at Delia Ross-Merlani once more—this time her inventory seemed to penetrate deeper than muscle, sinew and mien. Then, at last, the eyes of the two women met. And after what seemed like a very, very long time to Delia, Isabel Larsen nodded again, only once, this time in the direction of the barre. Delia at once stripped off her street clothes, put on leg warmers and toe shoes, and took her place at the barre behind her teacher. Without a word, Delia began to follow Isabel Larsen's movement into a first series of *pliés*.

Her teacup was empty and as she lifted her hand to signal the waiter, Delia could feel the muscles in her back beginning to tighten after the hours of effort she had expended that day. Then realizing that she had lost track of most everything as she had sat in the tearoom of the Stanhope Hotel, she asked the waiter, "What is the time?" At his reply, Delia rose quickly to her feet, ignoring the now considerable pain that this movement produced. She was late—Daniel was due at her hotel any moment. Delia grimaced. There would be another little scene about her bad habits and flighty ways. Well, *foutre!* She was not accustomed to punching a time clock. And if Dr. Daniel Elliot didn't like it—well, that was simply too bloody bad. Yes, sometimes she was tardy, but it was heaps better than being small and mean-spirited, she decided.

Hastily collecting her ballet bag and purse and parcels, Delia ran out of the hotel and into the car as Mr. MacPhee snapped the door smartly shut. She fidgeted with her hair, applied fresh lip gloss and then rammed her hat back on. At the Carlyle, she flung the door open on her own (bringing a look of consummate consternation to the faces of Mr. MacPhee and the doorman), and quickly ran inside. She impatiently tapped her foot in the elevator, afraid to glance at her watch to confirm that now she was more than thirty minutes late.

With a mixture of guilt, anger and remorse, Delia opened the door to her suite. A figure rose to meet her, and for a moment, Delia forgot everything and everyone. Everyone, that is, except the elegant ash-blond-haired woman extending a perfectly manicured hand.

"My darling," Lady Ross said to her daughter as she crossed the room to receive her embrace.

"And so I thought to myself, 'Well, since I shall be changing planes in New York, I'll stop off and see my Delia.' You look lovely, darling, *charmante*. A bit pale, perhaps."

"Thank you, Adela . . . I mean . . . yes, my Nice tan has faded. I'm so surprised to see you. Are you staying long? Where are you changing planes from? And to?"

"I came from Paris; you would not believe Yves' latest collection. *Merveilleux!* And I'm on my way to St. Lucia—Sir Lawrence has a house. 'Backgammon on the beach, Adela,' he said. And I thought, of course, Darley's foal won't arrive for at least a fortnight and oh . . . I spoke with Lady—"

"Where are you staying, Adela?" Delia asked quietly.

"For tonight, I've taken rooms at the Pierre. But really now, darling, you must hurry and change for dinner."

"Dinner?"

"We're dining with Ambassador Frebourg."

"Adela . . . I. . . ." Suddenly Delia became aware of Daniel's rising from his seat and approaching them. He kissed her softly on the forehead in a kind of tribute. "Your mother and I have already had a delightful chat, Delia. Enjoy your evening—I'll call you tomorrow." There was something strained and artificial in Daniel's voice which Delia had never heard before, and she looked wistfully at the door as it closed behind him.

"Such a nice young man. *Un Juif, non?* Well, hurry and dress, darling. We can have a very lovely, long tête-à-tête in the car."

And propelled by her mother's words, Delia hastened into her boudoir and gave herself up mindlessly to the efficient machinations of Mrs. MacPhee.

When Daniel Elliot opened his door somewhat after midnight, he found Viscountess Ross-Merlani, clad in a Halston gown and several magnificent pieces of emerald and diamond jewelry, with tears streaming down her face. Wordlessly, she walked into his arms. Daniel led her taut, sobbing body into his room, took off her jewels and then held her very tight to him.

"Why?" she said. "Why do they do this to me? Every time I manage to forget their existence, one of them barges into my life, picks me up, plays with me for a bit, and then without the slightest thought, puts me aside."

"Your father, too?"

She nodded. "Periodically I get one of Papa's famous 'summonses' to Italy and I run! I run! He wants to show off a new villa, a new yacht, a new mistress. . . ."

"Has it always been like this with your family?"

"No, sometimes I've been fortunate and they've completely forgotten my existence." Delia wiped away mascara streaks with the back of her hand. "And why do I give a damn? I'm nearly thirty years old! Why do I care if two selfish, superficial, empty-hearted people give me a tumble?"

Daniel sighed. "Because they're your parents."

"I genitori," she murmured. "Whence I take my beginnings."

"You can't run from it. Hard as you try to run from it—a tug on that umbilical cord brings you back," Daniel said.

"Is that what I'm trying to do? Run?"

"Sometimes I think you are. Sometimes I think, Delia, you're trying to outrun yourself."

She rested her head against his shoulder. "Why do you put up with me?"

"I love you," he said simply, kissing her fragrant hair.

She nodded, but was unable to offer the like in return. He knew this, and it made him clutch her ever more tightly to him.

"You're not the only one with family doings, however. My sister Linda called tonight. She's coming home for a visit again next week. Our attendance, *chez* Elliot, is required."

"Our?"

"Well, you'll want to meet Linda, and I've met your mother—it's time you met mine," he said lightly.

"Is it?" Delia asked, her tone serious.

"Yes," Daniel replied, turning her face up to look hard into her eyes.

"All right. But I've never really been brought home to meet Mama before. What do I wear?"

"Anything," he said with a smile, "except one of your damned hats."

"No hat!? I'll be positively naked, Daniel."

"Great," he said. "That's when I think you look your best." And with a soft laugh, he tumbled her back onto the bed.

Chapter Eighteen

Encore Une Fois

Daniel sat staring out the window of the coffee shop when he caught sight of his brunch date as she made her way down Second Avenue. Dressed in a simple pleated skirt, beige blouse, pearls and low-heeled shoes, Charlotte Frances Maitland looked the personification of English elegance. When she saw Daniel, her small face broke into a wide smile that made her look for all the world like Tenniel's happiest image of Alice.

"Morning, Daniel," Charlotte said as she sat down, "isn't it a lovely day?"

Daniel looked out the window and noticed the bright sunshine for the first time. "So it is. Thanks for mentioning it."

Charlotte smiled again. "Well, thank you for inviting me to brunch." Then she seemed to take in the coffee shop all in one quick glance.

"I hope this place is okay, Charlotte."

Charlotte laughed. "Oh, yes, it's fine for me. I'm not as particular about my surroundings as is my Lady Delia."

Daniel grinned. "Now that you've brought the subject up, that's precisely what I wanted to talk about. Not that I don't enjoy your company for its own sake, but . . ."

"Don't give it another thought, Daniel. I could tell from your carefully worded invitation that you wanted to talk about Delia."

Daniel frowned. "Did she tell you Adela blew into town last week?"

"Again?!" Charlotte said. "Ah well, that explains why Delia sounded so queer on the phone when I talked with her on Tuesday."

"Does her mother always upset her like this?"

"Oh, yes, usually. Both Adela and Papa have the unique capacity to make their daughter unhappy. And they always have. I don't think, however, either one of them realizes it or for that matter intends it. They're just selfish, self-absorbed people. They barely had time for each other."

"Then, where did Delia fit in?"

"She didn't; that was the problem. I think Adela felt a child would bind Federico to her. Aside from his passion for making money, he's also very occupied with his yacht, horses, and . . . women. But when Adela realized that he was as uninterested in his child as in his wife, she packed up and left. She's been traveling ever since."

"So Delia is a painful reminder to her mother of her failed marriage," Daniel said thoughtfully.

"Yes," Charlotte said. "And whether she knows it or not, Delia spends a great deal of time and energy either avoiding her parents or trying to get their attention."

"Which they seem to give sporadically."

"Yes . . . just enough to make her want it all the more," Charlotte said.

"Charming people," Daniel replied, his voice tight now with anger.

"Actually they are. That's the saddest part."

"How often does Delia see her father?" Daniel asked.

"Whenever he sends for her—not often."

"Not often enough?"

Charlotte nodded. "No. And they never take the trouble to really care about anything in her life. When Delia married Theo, Adela made this tremendous wedding at Rosemuir. There were more than eight hundred people—it was all over the society pages. Of course, Papa was there to give away the bride. Magda and I were Delia's attendants, matron and maid of honor, you see. I remember Magda commenting that everything *looked* so splendid. Like out of a fairy tale and with about as much reality to it. But when Delia got her doctorate, Magda and I and the Mac-Phees were the only attendants this time. My sister and I flew over for the ceremony; it was terribly impressive, you know. And though she won't admit it, Delia is *fiercely* proud of her ac-

159

ademic accomplishments. Her dissertation on the troubadours of medieval France was published and has been hailed as an important work. However, neither of her parents came to the ceremony, although at the time Adela was at Rosemuir which is not far from Cambridge. Instead, she sent her maid with a note of congratulations and a jade necklace she'd bought in the Orient. Papa had a magnificent chinchilla cape sent and, of course, a bottle of Perrier-Jouët."

"That was really swell of him."

"Yes well, instead of her parents giving of themselves to their daughter, they've given her beautiful things. That's why having beautiful things has become so very important to Delia. She clings to her jewels, houses, cars, because they represent something to her. She must always be the best and always have the best."

"I can't give her beautiful things," Daniel murmured softly.

"No, Daniel. Nor does she really need or want them. What Delia needs from you is, quite simply as the cliche goes, the things money can't buy." He nodded and Charlotte continued, "That won't be simple, though. Delia is often afraid to come out of that ivory tower of money and position that she's built for herself." There was a silence, and then Charlotte said, "In a way, my sister was, too."

"Magda? It doesn't sound to me like she was afraid of much."

Charlotte gave a sad smile. "Oh, but she was.

She was afraid to find out that people didn't really love her, so she tested the limits of their love over and over again. Until . . ."—Charlotte's eyes met Daniel's—"until her murder," she said with quiet authority.

"We can, on that point, at least agree to disagree," Daniel said.

"But we do agree on Delia?"

"Oh, yes," Daniel said firmly, "we love her. Again and again, we simply love her."

"Entrechat quatre, changement, entrechat quatre, changement. Bien, bien. Encore une fois." Just at the point that Delia thought she could not bear one more moment, the ballet mistress intoned, "All right, that's enough for today, ladies and gentlemen."

Amid the laughter and murmurs that accompany the end of ballet class, Delia limped her way into the dressing room. After only a week of study with Isabel Larsen, she had felt confident enough to return to company class with the New York Ballet Theatre.

In those years since she had danced with the Monte Carlo Ballet, Delia had lost more than her muscle tone and calluses. These she had quickly regained in this last week. But it was her place in the world of the professional performer that she now needed to reestablish. And this, she knew, might not be so easy.

She saw now those first nods of recognition

from many whom she had vaguely known several years ago. She knew, or at least knew of, a number of the people she had seen today in class. Women, no longer young, disillusioned, who knew that the magic moment when they would be singled out for stardom had passed them by. Resigned to their limitless routines of class, rehearsal, performance, she felt their appraisal of this returning member of their sisterhood and hoped that she had been designated as not much of a threat.

As she massaged her leg, Delia waited for an opportunity for conversation. A member of the corps she thought she recognized from her Royal Ballet School years gave her a tentative smile.

"Delia Something-Something? Right?"

"Delia Ross-Merlani. You're Carol Cranshaw."

The woman grimaced. "Carol Shawn now. Thought it would sound classier in reviews." She laughed self-deprecatingly.

Delia looked up at the other woman and suddenly frowned in what she hoped looked like even more pain than she actually felt.

"Not so easy to get back in shape—is it?" Carol Shawn asked sympathetically.

Delia shook her head as she gingerly removed the brand-new toe shoe she had worn today. No dancer would ever wear a new pair of *pointe* shoes to class, but Delia had deliberately done so. It had created just the right kind of visible swelling that she had hoped for. *"Merde!* What have I done?"

"Better ice that," Carol said, sitting down next to a now very gratified Delia. She had, she saw, reasoned correctly that her path would be smoother if she had appeared to blunder. "What on earth brings you back to the fold?" Carol asked.

"Oh," Delia said nonchalantly, "a man. It didn't work out. As I'm restless, pudgy and miserable, I decided that being in real pain wouldn't make much difference." The two women laughed, and there was now a sense of commiseration. "I'd forgotten, though, how *tough* you have to be for this. And thin!! God, I thought I was still in good shape till I came back to class today. Once I got my leotard on and got a gander at myself in the mirror, I was positively mortified."

Carol eyed Delia's form critically. "You don't look *too* bad," she said. "Maybe ten or twelve pounds."

Delia was in fact rather taken aback by this pronouncement but instantly strove to hide it. Although she had carefully prepared this part of the conversation, she hadn't exactly expected anyone to *agree* with her that she was overweight. She looked at the nearly emaciated child-like body of the other woman and told herself that only a dancer would want to look like the Little Match Girl.

"But it's so hard," Delia said. "I diet, or try to diet, and the weight just doesn't come off. If I don't eat, I won't have enough energy for class. If I do eat, I won't lose."

Carol nodded knowingly. "At twenty, the pounds melt away. At thirty. . . ." She shrugged.

"But you look simply marvelous," Delia said, infusing her voice with an enthusiasm she didn't feel. "How do you do it? What kind of diet are you on?"

"Oh, I can't diet. My life's too crazy. I take pills. They cut down your appetite, but give plenty of zip."

Delia chewed her lower lip in perfect imitation of Charlotte's look of helplessness. "Well, don'tcha know, I did ask my doctor and he said no go." And here Delia gave a perfect imitation of Dr. Mathews's tone of voice, "Pills are too dangerous."

"Doctors! Christ. There's only one 'doctor' in town who'll get you what you need."

"Oh?" Delia asked ingenuously. "I'm so out of touch with everything."

Carol smiled kindly. "There's this guy—called Dr. Don. He can get you anything—ups, downs, Valium, coke—anything. Used to be with the Westside Dance Troupe, I hear, and only deals for well . . . you know . . . for us."

Delia knew exactly what Carol meant by "us" and congratulated herself on being accepted once more into the world of that collective pronoun. She gently played with the ribbons of her toe shoe as she said, "I might want something a little out of the ordinary. Can he get it?"

"What he doesn't have—he makes. Has a lab of his own."

Voila!! Delia thought, the pain in her foot now a part of her triumph. "Where—how?"

"You know the Saturnalia—the club over on Twelfth Avenue?"

Delia nodded. She remembered Magda mentioning it to her when they had gone out dancing together in Paris . . . a private club for actors, models and dancers.

"That's where he is most nights," Carol said. "I go there pretty often. How about if I give you a call some night and we go together?"

"That would be great!" Delia gave Carol her telephone number, and they made tentative plans.

"See you in class tomorrow?" Carol asked as she gathered up her things.

"Uh, no. I can't tomorrow. I promised Mummy I would brunch with her," Delia said, easily bringing out this lie and briefly wondering what it would be like to have a mother that one called such an endearment. It was only as she stuffed her things into her bag and nodded to several women on her way out that Delia realized that come the next morning, she would most certainly be back in the studio of Isabel Larsen. She still felt some need, she knew, to continue to prepare herself—though precisely for what or against what was not entirely clear.

Chapter Nineteen

Feasting With Panthers

Daniel gave a sidelong glance at his lover and then brought his eyes back to the road ahead. She looked lovely, he thought, in a simple print dress ("Emanuel Ungaro," she had told him in response to his question) and discreet gold jewelry. And as requested, Delia wore no hat. But Daniel had now lovingly examined that profile enough times to read the subtle disquiet in it.

"A penny for your *pensée*," he asked.

"Where the devil are we?" Delia replied, and he knew she had not been thinking of this.

"Ocean Parkway, in the Flatbush section."

"And where did you say your parents lived?"

"In Sheepshead Bay," he said.

"In the bay?"

"Don't be cute, Professor." He suddenly realized she was nervous.

"Did you go to school around here?" Delia waved her hand in a vague direction.

"As a kid. But I went to a special high school in Manhattan."

"Then Cornell University and then . . . ?"

"I took my law degree first at Columbia and—"

"Your medical degree at Johns Hopkins," she said, remembering his tee shirt. Daniel nodded. "But you returned here, to your beginnings, as it were."

"Not quite," he said, making the turn onto Avenue R. Before he could elaborate on this point, the car pulled into the driveway of a small brick house in a block of houses that all looked to Delia's eye exasperatingly alike. "Ready?" he asked.

"Foutre!" Delia murmured, but gave a bright smile. Daniel kissed her nose in deference to the perfection of her applied lip gloss.

The door was opened by a small gray-haired man who had, Delia saw, Daniel Elliot's smile. "Hello, hello. Come in."

"Dad, this is Delia Ross-Merlani."

"Come in, young lady, come in."

"I'm glad to meet you, Mr. Elliot."

"I'm glad to meet you, too."

"Let me introduce you, Delia," Daniel said, as her eye took in the gathered semi-circle. Delia had an instant's recollection of arriving back at Rosemuir from boarding school that first time and the whole staff—from stableboy to butler—assembling to meet her at Adela's command.

How like her mother, she recalled, to sustain the forms of greeting even though she herself had not been there to welcome her daughter home. Delia put a bright smile on her face at the sound of Daniel's voice once again. "My sister Rachel . . . brother-in-law Steve, Jennifer aged six, Michael aged ten and as you can see, one on the way."

Delia shook hands and beamed appropriately. A tall, dark-eyed, striking-looking woman extended a hand to Delia and said simply, "I'm Linda," and then in a lowered voice, "prepare yourself—here comes Mom." Brother and sister exchanged a knowing glance—four dark eyes reflecting the same light, Delia saw.

"Gut yomtov. Gut yomtov," Mrs. Elliot said as she came into the living room.

Daniel shot his sister a quizzical look, and Linda murmured, *"Shavuos."*

"Hello, Mom," Daniel said, bending to kiss his mother. "I'd like you to meet Delia, Delia Ross-Merlani."

"How do you do, Mrs. Elliot. Thank you for inviting me."

Mrs. Ruth Elliot turned her huge, black gaze on her guest. In one swift glance, Delia felt those eyes had taken her in, and she knew at once she hadn't quite come up to measure. "I'm glad to meet *you,* Delia." Then in a ringing voice Mrs. Elliot commanded, "Please, everyone, to the table."

168

The entire family seemed to fall into previously prescribed places, and Delia found herself seated between Steve Roth and Linda Elliot. Mr. Elliot stood, recited the Hebrew blessing over the wine, and then they all sipped. Delia had never tasted such wine: it was dreadfully sweet and instantly assaulted her sensibilities. Then Mr. Elliot recited the blessing over the bread, a large twisted loaf of *challah,* and everyone echoed "Amen," only it sounded like "Aw-main" to Delia's ears.

All at once, Delia felt a flash of cold overwhelm her. *Where was she? Who on earth were these people? What were they saying?* These questions began to buzz round her mind, and she was unable to get herself clear of the sound. She looked frantically at Daniel, but somehow couldn't connect herself to him. He was talking to his elder sister, and although she could clearly hear his voice, the words seemed to be in a tongue she suddenly couldn't comprehend. Unable to find the toehold of the familiar, Delia felt herself beginning to sink.

"Christ, this wine is such shit!"

At Linda Elliot's words, Delia felt the clouds beginning to clear from her mind and turned to her. "What *is* this wine?"

"Kosher Concord Grape wine from Israel. Why oh, why, Lord, couldn't the chosen people have settled in Bordeaux?"

Delia gave a little smile and suddenly began to

feel better. In Linda's firm, soft voice, she had caught the familiar accents of her lover. When she looked up, Daniel's eyes were on her; she returned his smile. Just then, she was handed a plate piled high with small brown portions of an unknown food. They looked dreadful, she thought, but sensing Mrs. Elliot's eyes on her, she heaped two gingerly on her plate.

"Careful of the roast beef," Linda cautioned in a low voice, "my mother defines medium-rare as charred through. This, I think, she is calling 'well-done.'"

"What are these?" Delia asked, glancing at the newest arrivals on her plate.

"*Kishke,*" Mrs. Elliot piped up. "I suppose Delia's never eaten anything like it."

"Stuffed cow's intestine," Linda pronounced in Delia's ear.

Delia felt all eyes upon her. "Actually," she said, "my housekeeper, Mrs. MacPhee, makes a similar dish from her homeland called *haggis.*"

"Oh, really?" Mrs. Elliot rejoined coolly. "How nice."

"What does *haggis* taste like?" little Jennifer asked.

"A great deal like this as a matter of fact," Delia said thoughtfully as she chewed on the Jewish delicacy. She must remember, she noted, to tell Mrs. Mac that another culture had perfected an equally revolting use of the cow's insides as had the Scots.

"Michael came with me to *shul* today," Mr. Elliot said proudly. "Only a year of studies and he can *daven* as well as his grandfather."

"Daniel has told us that you know a number of languages," Rachel said, filling in the uncomfortable silence that had followed her father's remark. "I think that's such a remarkable talent. Which ones?"

"Ancient Greek, Latin, French. And Italian, of course."

"Italian, of course?" Mrs. Elliot said.

"Well, yes, my father is Italian. Although I was raised in England, I also spoke Italian as a child."

"And what do you do with all these languages, Miss . . . uh . . . Delia?" Henry Elliot said, a little embarrassed.

Delia gave him her softest smile. He was shy, she could see, and slightly uncomfortable in her presence. His fumbling over the correct way to address her reminded Delia of the man's son and his own shy, diffident ways. She would like Henry Elliot, she decided.

"Well, I used to teach courses in Medieval Studies at Newnham College . . . at Cambridge University."

"And now?"

"Now I'm visiting friends here in New York."

"And where do your parents live?" Mrs. Elliot asked, making no attempt to disguise her inter-

171

rogation.

"My father lives in Milan—and my mother's house is in Surrey . . . that's south of London," Delia said carefully.

"You have an unusual name—Ross-Merlani," Mrs. Elliot said, her voice actually pungent with criticism.

Delia had, soon after her first visit to Magda in America, accustomed herself to the difficulties a hyphenated name presented. She had learned to be flippant when the occasion demanded or to give a thorough explanation for her seemingly unusual surname. In the carefully modulated voice of the instructor she began, "My mother's family is Ross; my father's Merlani. As I am to inherit my mother's lands and title, I follow the European custom and use both names."

"*Title?*" Mrs. Elliot's eyes opened wide.

Delia saw Daniel's face instantly darken and could even sense Linda's dismay. "Y-y-yes," she said, stammering at what she now gathered must be a misstep. She realized, however, she had no place to go except forward. "My mother is the Countess of Ross."

"Fancy-schmantzy," Mr. Elliot said lightly.

His wife's face, however, reflected no good humor. "I see." And turning to her son she said, "How lovely, Daniel, that the first young woman you bring home to meet us in nearly a year should turn out to be such an *interesting person.*"

Delia realized with surprise that Mrs. Elliot had made the words "interesting person" sound like an undeniable epithet. She did not hear Daniel's reply if he gave one. His mother, however, her investigation complete, allowed a new topic to be introduced.

The rest of the evening seemed to pass in a blur to Delia. Mrs. Elliot did not speak to her again. Several times, she addressed inquiries to her son, "Would your friend like some potatoes, do you think?" "Does your friend want some more wine?" Each time she was mentioned in the third person, Delia felt herself diminished. Before she left, Delia again made polite comments and shook hands with everyone. Mrs. Elliot expressed pleasure at making her acquaintance, and Delia murmured like sentiments. To Linda's encouraging smile, Delia said, "I'm at the Carlyle. Call me and we'll have lunch." The other woman nodded assuringly.

Back in the car, however, the lovers retraced their previous route amid a charged silence. Finally, Delia said, "I should much prefer the axe to fall, you know."

"What?" Daniel said shortly.

"Say it, Daniel. Detail the scope of my *crime*."

With a sudden jerk of the wheel, he crossed two lanes and brought the car to a lurching halt at a bus stop. "It seems to me that being half-Jewish, half-Catholic, half-English, half-Italian, half-dancer, half-professor and half-whatever-the-fuck-else you are, Delia, would make you feel superior enough to those people. Was it really necessary to parade your heraldic colors for them as well? How insignificant did you have to make them feel?"

Delia sat in stony silence. "Oh, let me hold my tongue," she thought, "please don't let him provoke me to speak."

"They tried, for my sake, to welcome you to their home and to extend their hospitality—meager as it might be compared to the likes of the Swiss Ambassador. But *your ladyship* simply mounted her high horse and rode right on over them."

Pushed past her furthest point of endurance, Delia exploded. "How dare you? How dare you castigate *me* after that exhibition of insensitivity? Did it ever occur to you how awkward and adrift I might feel in being greeted in a language I do not know, with words I do not understand? You might have told me today was a holy day—I might have at least been prepared to wish your family a happy holiday. I've never heard of '*Shavuos.*' I didn't know if it was a day of celebration or mourning or what."

"*Shavuos?* Oh, it's a feast . . . feast of the harvest or something . . . not a big thing really."

"No, Daniel. Not to you. But I don't understand any of their ways. *Gut yomtov, shul, daven.* The food, the talk, the very tenor of the gathering was geared to make me feel excluded.

Your mother didn't ask about anything we might have had in common. She only tried to point up our differences."

Suddenly all of Delia's efforts to the contrary were in vain as she felt herself begin to cry. "Don't you think I know that it matters to you? Don't you think I *wanted* them to like me? Accept me? Dinner with the family and once more I'm pushed outside with my nose pressed to the glass. Why didn't you see, Daniel? Why didn't you understand? Was it because you, too, were so busy seeing *our* differences?"

Daniel reached out a tentative hand to her, but she shook herself free. They drove home in a stiff silence which Daniel finally broke as the Carlyle doorman assisted Delia out. "I'll call you, Delia . . . and . . ."

She didn't wait, however, to hear his last remark, but hurried back to her own ground.

Chapter Twenty

Brave New World

Delia began with a *chassé* to give impetus to the jump. Then without pause, she executed a *grand jeté en tournant* ending with her back leg extended and her arms opening into a first *arabesque*. Isabel nodded, and Delia executed the movements over and over again. Finally her teacher murmured, *"Bien,"* and Delia held the final pose. Then after a beat, she came back into fifth position and waited.

Isabel Larsen stood for several moments gazing at her student. Both women looked, to the casual glance, rather similar—dressed in black leotards, pink tights, leg warmers and toe shoes, their hair pulled back into ballet buns. But there was no tightness in the older woman's body while Delia held hers as taut as a high tension wire. Finally Isabel spoke, "If you continue to dance as you have this morning, Delia, you will surely injure yourself."

Stung by these words, Delia whirled around

to face her teacher. "But how? I have worked very hard on correct placement, Madame. And you yourself are always saying how it is incorrect placement that leads to injuries in ballet."

Isabel steadfastly eyed Delia once again. "But of course. If one is out of alignment, there is always a terrible risk. But I believe also that the body can be in perfect place and something of the self can be what is out of alignment. And *that* can be even more dangerous, Delia. Your placement today has been excellent as far as your body is concerned. But your heart . . . ah your heart, Delia, is seeming to drive you over some edge." She came forward and took Delia's face between her two hands. "Do you not know that every vibration in your deepest being is reflected in your dance? What on earth is troubling you?"

In the hours and hours that Delia had spent in the studio studying with this great teacher, Isabel had touched her many, many times in order to correct the placement of Delia's foot or hand, or to turn her torso ever so slightly in form. But never once, Delia knew, had her teacher ever exhibited the tiniest sign of approbation much less affection. Now Delia stood for just a moment opposite the other woman, and then she softly began to cry. "Oh, Madame, I don't understand. I don't understand. It went all wrong and I don't even know why."

"What went all wrong?"

"I went to visit the family of someone . . . someone who is coming to mean a great deal to me. And they hated me! No. Not hated me. They didn't *let me in*. They shut me out. I'm always feeling shut out, Madame. I keep trying to open my heart, and I'm always being shut out."

Isabel Larsen dropped her hands to her sides. "And this someone? You wish to open your heart to this someone?"

"Yes," Delia said simply.

Isabel took Delia by the hand and led her over to the barre, and side-by-side they stood in front of the mirror. "Do you remember, Delia, that first day you came into a ballet studio for the first time? How old were you?"

"I was eight."

"And Madame Nicolaeva was teaching the class?"

"Yes," Delia said, feeling herself now back in that place and in that time.

"I remember, too, my first class. Mine was with Madame Kazinska. I remember how much I wanted to be so very good. And how difficult it seemed at first. I knew little French, less English, no Italian, nor Russian. And the terms and the very place were so unfamiliar to me. All I knew is that I wanted to dance. But during those early times, I only felt like I was on the outside watching everyone else in the mirror."

Then in an altered voice Isabel said, "Fifth position, *demi-plié,* one and two . . ." and instantly both women moved in unison. "And now, you see. It is so much a part of who we are that our heart opens easily—and we embrace the air in joy each time." She turned to her pupil and put a hand on her shoulder. "It can only come in time. This I have learned, my dear, this I have learned . . . if you have a willing heart, you will find your place in whatever worlds you enter."

Delia gazed back at the older woman for a long moment. Then she slowly fell into a deep, deep curtsy such as she had been taught to do back at the ballet school so many years before. "Thank you, Madame," she said and came back up only as she felt her teacher's hand beneath her chin raising her up, and up, into her place once again.

"How ugly was the scene between you?"

Delia paused in her perusal of the Shun Lee Dynasty menu and looked up at her interlocutress. They were in a restaurant that served "the best Chinese food outside of Beijing" according to her companion. The Elliot siblings, Delia had noted, seemed to deal in culinary superlatives.

Her ladyship took a moment to consider the question and the poser. It was more, Delia decided, than the fact that Linda reminded her of Daniel. No, at this moment that might be a liability rather than a credit, she thought ruefully. She saw that she was forming a genuine liking for Linda Elliot in the way of her younger days. She liked the other woman's apparent sense of humor and sense of self.

"I'll trade confidences," Delia said in a measured tone. "You tell me about what followed our departure."

Linda made a face. "We'd better order first." In a peremptory way, not unlike her brother's quiet authority, Linda gave crisp instructions to the waiter, barely attending to Delia's murmured preferences.

The two young women made quite a pretty picture for the late lunch crowd. Linda was clearly the more classically beautiful of the two, with a tangle of heavy, red-gold waves and the magnetic Elliot eyes. She was taller than her companion and less angular, more womanly. But she dressed and carried herself with a nonchalance in marked contrast to Delia's studied effects. Linda wore a skirt and shirt in the style Delia liked to call "California *Cacatura*." To the initiated eye, Delia's Gianfranco Ferre suit and Claude Montana hat would be the apotheosis of good taste. Yet each woman attracted her share of admiring glances: the striking Linda as well as the deceptively cool-looking Delia.

180

The wintermelon soup arrived, and both ate in silence for several moments. Then Linda put aside her spoon and began to munch on the noodles from the bowl between them. She signalled the waiter. "Bring me another scotch and soda." She looked inquiringly at Delia, who shook her head.

"Okay. Listen, and I'll try to explain. My parents have and have always had big plans for Dan. That's not the same as being interested in his happiness. You must understand their way of thinking. Rach is okay—I'm a bit of a washout, but out of sight and out of town so that's okay, too. Danny is the golden boy . . . a doctor. But he's not turning out as they had hoped."

"You mean by not marrying Robin?"

"Oh, you know about her? Good. No—it's more than that. Dan got a string of scholarships—went to real swell schools and look what he's doing with his talents."

Delia considered and then said, "I don't think I understand."

"What does Dan make—sixty thousand? Seventy maybe? In my parents' world, that's nuts. With his credentials, he could be making at least four times that in private practice."

"Does that matter so much?"

"To my parents? It means everything! Listen, my grandparents came over from Russia in steerage without a *kopek* to their names. They were poor, real poor. They slaved in sweat shops to get their kids off the Lower East Side. Sheepshead Bay is one rung up on the ladder. This is our legacy. We're all expected to continue the climb. Especially Dan as he is the boy."

Delia thought this over. "And Daniel understands, lives with this idea?"

"Sure, we all do. I stay as far away as possible so I don't have to read the disappointment in their eyes. Poor Danny gets the crap on a more regular basis."

"What else do they expect of him aside from making a great deal of money?"

"They want him to live out their dream of middle-class splendor and security. That goes back to our great-grandparents living in little hovels on someone else's land."

"They wanted Robin," Delia murmured.

"Oh, yes. Or one of her prototype. Jewish, bright, pretty—right family, right background, right ideas—just like theirs."

"So I was not a success."

Linda laughed and dug into the Lake Tung Ting Shrimp. "Ah—no. You were like something from Mars to them. I tried to convince them that you were half-Jewish and well-educated and that it could be worse. But my mother wailed for several hours. You are 'the final nail in the coffin of Dan's life.' "

"Is that a direct quote?"

Linda nodded.

Delia felt slightly sick inside. This vision of herself was an unbearable rubbing of an already open wound in her self-esteem.

"How did Danny take it?" Linda asked.

"Not well. He accused me of snobbery and condescension. He didn't see how difficult it was for me, and we had an awful row." Then she murmured, "Our first."

"Christ — sometimes even the smartest men are such schmucks. Between him and Manaro there's scarcely an ounce of sense when it comes to handling volatile situations — like parents."

Delia looked up, surprised at the vehemence of the other's tone.

Linda colored slightly. "Danny didn't tell you about Pete and me? Well, you'd get it sooner or later. When we were young — back when I was in college — we lived together for about a year. Between my mother and Mama Manaro there was enough noise to bring down the walls of Jericho." She paused. "Enough to crumble our thin citadel." Then she smiled brightly. "But that was ages ago. Hopefully we've all grown up a little. And I think it showed my brother his mistake with Robin — 'the bird' Pete used to call her." Linda smiled fondly. "He's basically a good man — Manaro. We're still friends. I hope

183

he finds that kind of special woman who can make him happy."

Delia smiled in return, and unbidden, a perplexing image of Charlotte and Pete Manaro crossed her mind. Linda signalled for the check which the two women split without any further ado.

"How long will you be in town?" Delia asked.

"Just a couple more days, I'm afraid. Off to your neck of the woods. I'm attending some seminars at the University of London. I have to get over there and find a place to camp out for a couple of weeks."

"You'll do no such thing! I'll give you the keys to my flat and you'll make yourself at home there. In fact, I'll talk with Mrs. Mac, my housekeeper, tonight and have her arrange all the details. I'm sure she'll get you right settled, my lassie."

"Thanks—that's a lovely offer and I'm delighted to accept." The two women exchanged warm looks, and Delia was certain that this indeed spelled the beginning of a true friendship. "Are you planning on being in New York much longer?"

"I don't actually know," Delia murmured. "It depends."

"Listen, Delia. I know Dan's been a jerk, but he's really in love with you."

Delia nodded. "Yes, I know."

184

"Are you in love with him?"

"I don't know that, Linda. I've spent much of my life, trowel in hand, making fortifications. It's hard now to scale them."

"Especially if you're still building?" Linda asked softly.

Delia smiled, and the two women walked out arm-in-arm to the car.

"I'm meeting my mother at Bloomies, so I'll hike a bit. Listen, I hope you two work things out. I, for one, think you make a great couple." Linda and Delia embraced and then parted.

"What direction, Miss Delia?" Mr. MacPhee asked.

Delia shook her head slowly. "I don't really know, Mr. Mac," she said softly. "I don't know at all."

Chapter Twenty-one

Night Work

"A message for you from a 'Carol,' Miss Delia." Delia could hear the distaste in Mrs. MacPhee's voice and wondered what verbal crime of Carol's could have prompted such instant dislike. "She said," Mrs. MacPhee continued, "that she would meet you at the Saturnalia at eleven—and you should wear your 'bestest jazz shoes and disco pants.' What in the name of St. Andrew are disco pants?"

"A wee bit like plus-fours, only tighter and shinier. Well, it seems I'm going out tonight, *mia cara*. You and the mister can dine by yourselves—I'll have a room service something or other."

After shooing out the MacPhees, Delia picked at her Bucheron tart for a time, took a long bath and then read several chapters in Marguerite Duras's latest novel. At twenty minutes past eleven, she slipped into the stiletto heels and Betsey Johnson dress she had acquired several days before in anticipation of this foray.

From her makeup case, Delia extracted several new pots of colors and artfully over-made her face. Then she unbound her fine, straight black hair and brushed it down her back. The insertion of two rhinestone-studded haircombs completed her carefully constructed facade. She stood for a moment with the bottle of Je Reviens in her hand before applying a generous spray. Funny, she thought, how some things still held one. This scent, which Adela had always worn, had become so ingrained in Delia's mind as a little girl with the image of a woman that she had as a matter of course used it herself. Looking again at the bottle in her hand, she resolved now to find a perfume signature of her own—one that Daniel might like. And then she recalled that what Daniel Elliot might or might not like might or might not matter to her anymore. Hastily, Delia put the bottle and these thoughts away, tossed on a satin jacket and sailed out of her suite.

The cab dropped her off at the Saturnalia near midnight. In the few minutes it took her to find Carol, Delia accustomed herself to the loud bass beat, whirling colors, smoke, and smells of scent, liquor and predatory sweat. Carol introduced her to a small group of regulars, a few of whom now had moderately familiar faces.

During the next hours, Delia danced, drank and strutted with the best of them. But all the time, she felt this peculiar chill on the edge of

187

her nerves. Might this become her life—this mindless hedonistic frenzy? Could dope, dreams and disappointments become the filler for her ever-searching soul?

A girl flashed by suddenly, somewhat graceless, but with a blur of blond not unlike Magdalene's. Had she found some peace? Delia wondered. Had Magda found some peace before her end? And again, Delia heard her friend's voice, more than ten years before, still fresh, reciting,

> " 'My love is of a birth as rare
> As 'tis for object strange and high:
> It was begotten by despair
> Upon impossibility.' "

Something like panic seized Delia then. And in the haze of noise and bodies, she saw black eyes driving her back, back, back into the crowd. Whose eyes? Mrs. Elliot's? Her father's? Daniel's? Or was it merely the boundless reflected depths of her own?

"Delia."

She started. The sound of her name brought her back to reality as would a spray of cold fine rain upon her face. "Yes?"

"Dr. Don isn't here tonight. But I found out where we can find him. Want to go?" Delia nodded, and miraculously, it seemed, they were out in the cool night air of the Hudson. Carol hailed a cab and gave an address. Delia raised an inquiring brow as she recognized the name of the fashionable, newly elected legislator.

They were soon let into a plush penthouse whose present assemblage of individuals and ambiance did not markedly differ from the one they'd just left. Carol nodded to people here and there and finally ferreted out Dr. Don standing with a glass of wine in his hand next to what Delia knew was an original Joan Miró painting. After a brief explanation and testaments to Delia's discretion, Carol left them alone.

"What can I do for you?"

Delia studied this interesting figure for a minute. Dr. Don was about her own age, very handsome, very well dressed and very businesslike. "What do you do in the daytime?" she asked in reply.

He laughed and said vaguely, "I sell commodities to willing buyers. What do you do in the daytime?"

"Try to make it through to the nights," she said, meeting his gaze with one in exact imitation of Charley's look of wide-eyed wonderment. She had cultivated this particular presentation during the hours of her investigation into Magda's missing prescription. She saw now that it stood her in fine stead as the dealer's eyes lit up in appreciation. Having made her impression Delia hastened to add, "I'm trying to score some stuff for my boyfriend."

"What kind of 'stuff'?"

"He's been real raggey lately and trying to diet. I want to get him a bit of dexadrine, you see. A kind of special gift. But I don't want the pills to be recognized. I want them to look like antacids."

"Sounds strange, but I've heard stranger."

"He works for a real straight outfit. I want him to be able to just pop a pill and claim it's for the three martini lunches." She paused. "I was told by a friend that you do make up special orders."

"Who's your 'friend'?"

Delia heard Dr. Don's peculiar emphasis of this last word and firmed up her guard just a bit. Carefully she said, "Came to see you a while back. Wanted reds made into little white pills. At least I think he said he came to you."

Dr. Don's face suddenly went completely blank; Delia was more than well prepared for this turn of events. From her purse, she took out five Krugerrands and began to roll them back and forth and back and forth slowly in her delicate hand. "If you made up an order like that—maybe you could describe my friend. See, you know, if it's the same chappie."

Dr. Don was staring at the coins in her hand. Then with hard eyes he said, "Who the hell are you, lady?"

Coolly, Delia said, "I'm not a cop." And just at that moment, she realized how proud she was of the way in which she had acquired all these little Americanisms. "This is a private settlement." She returned his glance now with that look she had inherited which combined Adela's *noblesse oblige* and Papa's complete and absolute occupation of position.

After a moment, Dr. Don shrugged, and extended his hand. Delia dropped the coins into it, and he pocketed them. Then he said, "Tall guy, red beard. Met him at the Saturnalia a couple of times about eight, nine months ago, might have been a year. I don't keep very accurate books."

"A name?"

The dealer laughed. "Winston Churchill," he said dryly.

Carol stuck her head in and said, "Ready?" Delia nodded and Carol asked, "Did you get what you wanted?"

"Your friend got what she came for." Dr. Don gave a low laugh and turning an appreciative gaze once more on Delia asked, "What did you say your name is . . . Miss . . . Miss . . . ?"

"Sharp . . . Becky Sharp," Delia said as she sailed out of the room giving her sweetest smile of dismissal.

What *was* that noise, she wondered, and then perceived the ringing of the phone. She looked at the clock: 2:11 P.M. Right. Sometime around dawn, she had returned to her hotel and left word not to be disturbed until two. The phone still rang. She groped and grabbed the receiver. "Hello."

"Hello, Delia." Daniel's voice was like ice suddenly applied to her spine, and she bolted awake. They had not spoken since the night of the dinner at his parents'. "Have a pleasant evening?" he queried, but she heard no urbanity in his voice.

"Yes. Why?"

"Just a friendly inquiry. Got in rather late—or quite early, I think. Or are you just getting in now?"

God, she was too tired for a scene, Delia thought. "We've been through this before. I don't punch a time clock, Daniel."

"That's always been obvious." His voice had gone from testy to nasty. "I thought last night that we could try to work things out. I called to invite you for dinner or drinks or a nightcap. Finally, I would have settled for breakfast, but it appears her ladyship was otherwise engaged through the night."

"Nor do I account for my time to anyone. As the proverbial bird, Daniel . . . I am free."

"Just what I've been thinking. Magda Maitland's kind of freedom. *Birds* of a feather, perhaps."

"Oh, *foutre!*" she said, slamming the receiver down. "I owe explanations to no one," she shouted at the phone. "No one! Not even you. Not even you," she repeated, crying softly now into her empty hands.

Chapter Twenty-two

The Caucus-Race

"Minchione! I hate the rain." Delia sat staring out the window of her suite. "You would think all those bloody years in England would have accustomed me to it."

She stretched catlike on the sofa and began to twirl her hair round her fingers. There were a thousand things she could do today. Take a ballet class, lunch at Olympe, see the new Almodovar, fly off to Paris, Rome, the moon. Delia's fingers tugged at her hair.

Perhaps, she thought, it was time to move on. Perhaps she had been reading too much into the evidence about Magda. Oh, yes, the information from Dr. Don had been intriguing and rather gratifying . . . but really this whole thing was beginning to seem a mite silly, wasn't it? *Grand Guignol* melodrama and its attendant murder was surely not the only possible explanation for Magda's death. What had made her imagine that she was cut out to be a detective? Perhaps this whole business with Magda had only been an excuse to stay in New York . . . an excuse to see Daniel.

"Right," she decided, "I'll fly to London tomorrow, be at Rosemuir the next day. I'll go riding . . . yes . . . and read . . . and garden . . . find myself. Lose myself."

Sometimes I think, Delia, you're trying to outrun yourself. She heard Daniel's words resounding in her head.

"You need a real occupation," Mr. MacPhee said, looking up from his copy of *The Times* and breaking in abruptly on Delia's thoughts. "That's what you need."

"She needs a husband and a proper home; that's what she needs," Mrs. MacPhee mumbled over her knitting.

Delia picked up a seat cushion and threw it at the heavy, gray braided hair, deliberately missing it. "Oh, be quiet! Both of you! I'm so bloody bored."

"Why don't you call Miss Charlotte?"

"Charlotte's at school. She's taking some ludicrous course—Urban Sociology—God knows what put that into her head—at something called 'The New School.' God. God!"

"Then why not . . . ?"

Delia stood up, and the MacPhees, in concerned silence, watched as she strode round the suite. She grabbed her bag, mackintosh and hat. Then, ramming her fists into her pockets, she announced, "I'm going out."

194

Mr. MacPhee jumped to his feet. "I'll bring the car round."

"Sit still!" Delia commanded. "I am going to walk."

"In the rain?" Mrs. MacPhee asked anxiously.

"Yes. It's supposed to be good for one's complexion," she snapped. Then Delia turned and went out, slamming the door behind her.

She walked aimlessly down Madison Avenue, looking now and then in shop windows, making and discarding mental purchases. She knew why she was so edgy and truly regretted taking her mood out on the darling Macs.

Oh, damn him! Why was he able to upset her so? Why was he able to get at her in a way no one had ever done? Yes, he was attractive. Bright, yes. Clever? Well, yes, but she had known many bright, clever people.

But none, she knew, like Dr. Daniel Elliot. None whose look and touch could put up her guard as his did. And none for whom she wanted more to take down her guard.

Delia caught a glimpse of herself reflected in the window of Betsey Bunky and Nini. A woman, not beautiful, but clearly striking, of indeterminate age, carelessly attired in good things, wet, angry and, she noticed, crying.

Hailing a cab, Delia got in and said, "New York Public Library."

The main reading room of the New York Public Library smelled like old glue to Delia. It was not an unpleasant smell, rather it was comforting, even familiar. Like the smell of the library at Cambridge.

Out of an almost forgotten instinct, Delia settled herself down, fished her notebook and pen from her bag and turned her mind to the solving of a problem. At the top of a fresh page in her notebook she wrote:

FACTS

1. At the time of her death, M had suffered from a series of gastric attacks which did not precipitate her death. Elevated white count.

2. Autopsy did not give any conclusive evidence for the attacks.

3. She was taking what she thought were Ortho Novum birth control pills, but the pills were in fact Seconals.

4. She had left Ned.

5. She was living with Jason Howland.

Delia looked at this list of facts, none of which separately seemed like much, she thought. But put together, they might yield a discernible design if only she could figure out how to work the warp and woof.

Again heading a separate page, she wrote:

MEDICAL EVIDENCE

1. M had a series of seizures which led to respiratory failure and death.

2. Secobarbital sodium, in small amounts, was found in her body.

3. She had an elevated white count during her attacks and at the time of her death.

Delia started to cross out this last point as repetitious when her hand stopped above the page. It was a *lead,* she realized. One that she had never properly followed up on. She recalled Charlotte's description of her sister's attacks: "She was in dreadful pain." And Dr. Mathews reported that Magda had described the pain as "violent spasms . . . up near her heart."

On a clean page, Delia began:

THE ATTACK

1. Sudden

2. Episodic (monthly?)

3. Terrible pain

4. Elevated white count

Something about this last list satisfied her. It was short and succinct. To the point. And then without warning, Delia's eyes suddenly blurred:

"Something horrible happened, Mags," Delia *said, addressing her friend as they sat side-by-side in the gazebo at Rosemuir, Charlotte having fallen asleep in the late-afternoon sun.*

Magda nodded, her beautiful face looking sweet and stern. " 'O pure of heart! thou need'st not ask of me/ What this strong music in the soul may be!' " she recited.

Delia's vision cleared as she jumped to her feet. She hastened over to the librarian's desk. After several moments of consultation, Delia returned to her place armed with *Behr's Textbook of Medicine*. In addition, she kept a copy of *Gray's Anatomy* and *Stedman's Medical Dictionary* at her elbow.

She opened *Behr's Text* and turned to the section on the cardiovascular system and began to read. In spite of her Greek and Latin standing her in good stead and her frequent reference to *Gray's* and *Stedman's,* this section took most of the day.

Delia returned to her suite, her head spinning, feeling weary but satisfied. She hadn't learned much, only enough to know that Magda had not suffered from any cardiac complaint. But this first taste of knowledge nourished her.

"Any calls?" she asked Mrs. MacPhee as she

downed her dinner of *gigot d'agneau rôti* and *ra-tatouille.*

"No," Mrs. MacPhee said, watching her mistress's face for signs of distress and surprised not to find any.

For the next three days, Delia's life followed much of the same pattern. The early morning found her at Isabel Larsen's studio for several hours of ballet; by noon she had ensconced herself in the reading room of the New York Public Library and begun to plow her way through another section of *Behr's Text.* She made notes, checked ideas and kept a list of things to discuss. Discuss with whom, she did not let her mind consider.

The fourth afternoon, another wet, gray day, found her ladyship seated with the accustomed texts before her, but she was not reading. In spite of the many pep talks she had given herself, Delia's spirits were starting to flag. Aside from acquiring an almost indecently thorough knowledge of human ills, she was beginning to doubt if she was pursuing a worthwhile line of investigation.

A clap of sharp thunder made her start in her seat. She grinned and gave a metaphorical nod to the gods. With a brisk shake of her mental framework, Delia Ross-Merlani once more applied herself to the job.

She turned to the section headed "Gastro-Intestinal System" and gave a slight shudder. Delia had a morbid, although carefully concealed, dislike of odors. Simply the thought of an unpleasant whiff could start her stomach churning. This dislike, bordering on phobia, had kept her attention away from this particular section in spite of the obvious relevance to Magda's case. Delia hadn't minded the cardiac, respiratory or endocrine systems. These internal mechanisms had even fascinated her to some degree.

However, she felt an instinctive revulsion as her eyes began to read through the gastro-intestinal system. But ever the good scholar, she turned to "The Alimentary Canal" and started to read, beginning with "Halitosis."

After an hour, Delia thought she might take a break and get a cup of coffee, but the thought of the bilious liquid deterred her. She concluded it was necessary to complete "Diseases of the Liver" before embarking on such a course.

"The Porphyrias," Delia read and paused. "What an interesting word," she reflected, and ran it through her bank of etymological knowledge. "From the Greek, πόρφυρος perhaps? Purple . . . yes . . . it means purple. Wasn't there a poem about someone named Porphyria? Matthew Arnold maybe . . . or Browning . . . one of that ilk. Porphyria's . . . Something. Porphyria's Lament? No, Lover . . . yes, that's it . . . Porphyria's Lover," she thought. Delia couldn't remember just then the particulars of the poem, only that she had thought it a bit nasty when she had studied it at school.

Delia went back to her notes. Rare disorder . . . attacks of acute abdominal pain . . . high white count . . ."

Suddenly it seemed to Delia as if she could not sit still one moment longer. Her energies were super-charged. Frantically, she scribbled page after page in her notebook. Then she jumped to her feet. People glanced up at her as she tried to stifle her flailing limbs, but her excitement was too much—almost sexual in intensity.

She quickly ran out of the room and out of the building. She stood for a moment at the top of the steps, wanting to roar back at the stone lions before her. Soon drenched by the continual downpour, Delia laughed aloud. There should have been a bright sun, she knew, or perhaps a rainbow to greet this discovery. But instead, the perverse literary moment made her exult even in being splashed by a passing car as she dashed to the curb to hail a cab.

She seethed in excitement during the ride downtown. Flinging a fifty dollar bill at the astonished driver, Delia raced into the Medical Examiner's Office and presented herself at the reception desk.

Only as she felt the eyes of others on her did Delia realize how absurd she must seem. Muddy, dripping and wild-eyed, she had rushed in and demanded to see the assistant medical examiner. The receptionist was inquiring in a snippy tone about appointments.

Delia composed herself, took a deep breath and began to speak in her most Hunt-Ball accents. "I'm the Viscountess Ross-Merlani.

Please ask Dr. Elliot if he might spare me a moment."

Seemingly cowed by Delia's title and manner, the receptionist called Daniel's office and, with a look of sour surprise, finally told Delia, "Go right in, second door on your left."

Delia quickly gave her most condescending smile and then dashed into Daniel Elliot's office. His look of formal welcome turned to shock when he beheld her.

Delia took Daniel's face between her two wet hands and kissed him, thrusting her tongue deep into his throat. She felt his surprise, momentary rebellion and final surrender: Daniel folded his arms about her.

Delia looked up at him as Daniel pushed the wet hair off her face, looking deeply into her eyes. "I know how Magda died . . . how she was murdered. I may even know by whom. I'll be at your place tonight at seven, sharp."

Daniel nodded and wordlessly watched her walk from the room. And he knew absolutely, as he had not known anything in his life before, that he would never let this woman walk out of his life again.

Chapter Twenty-three

Patching Together

Daniel sat propped up against the pillows, sipping Remy Martin and reading the latest issue of *The New Yorker*. Delia lay stretched out naked, her head upon his loins, her eyes intent upon the book in her hands, *The Victorian Poets*. Every now and again, Daniel's hand would slide lazily across her thin shoulder and caress her breasts.

It was late at night, that time when lovers of some standing but not great duration have spent their passions and feel comfortable in their own skins and with each other. Now having finished all the reviews, Daniel glanced down at Delia. He adored her profile; she looked ugliest in profile, he had decided. The beautiful eyes, unseen, could not mitigate the hard nose and aggressive full lips. "I love you," he said without hesitation, though he could hear something of his own astonishment still.

Delia smiled up at him, wishing she could reassure him in some way, yet very much aware that the person she needed most to reassure was herself. Then she sat up and poured each a second snifter of cognac. "Listen," she said, "this is a story, a case history, a murder." Daniel nodded.

"Two years ago, Magda began to have episodic gastric attacks. All of the medical tests were negative. No ulcer, no gallstones. Her appendix was removed. Yet her attacks continued off and on. Last year the attacks started to come more often—then almost regularly. Magda was hospitalized January 12, February 8, March 7—every *twenty-eight days*."

Daniel sat up and looked at her. "Don't tell me you buy Dr. Mathews's—?"

"No, don't be daft. Shhh! Just wait." Delia's voice took on a lilting, sing-song rhythm, and she saw that Daniel had begun to listen as though mesmerized. "All the medical reports stated that she had pain, vomiting and an elevated white count. Magda said the pain was high up, under her breasts, a hard squeezing pain. The post mortem showed traces of Seconal . . . a barbiturate." Daniel nodded, intent, but he said nothing.

"Finally there were the seizures which killed her. Was Magda menstruating at the time of her death?" Daniel nodded again, and Delia let a slow grin spread across her generous mouth.

She took her notebook from her bag and began very slowly "These are the specifics of acute intermittent porphyria: affects mostly women in their twenties and thirties; attacks are precipitous;

severe abdominal pain; seizures; psychiatric symptoms including 'hysterical' behavior. Attacks may be triggered by estrogens, menstruation, infection, pregnancy, and barbiturates."

All the color had drained from Daniel's face. "Jesus Christ—acute intermittent porphyria! Of course—all the pieces fit!"

Very gently Delia asked, "Then why didn't any of her doctors see it?"

Daniel gave her a smile, grateful for this unexpected display of tact. "It's so rare a disease, Delia, and the test is complicated. I remember studying it in medical school. Our professor told us of one case—a real gruesome story—went undiagnosed for years. The patient kept coming to the hospital with attacks. Poor woman, no one believed she was ill."

"Originally Magda's attacks were spontaneous—brought on by menstruation?"

"Probably. Porphyria is a metabolic defect which causes the production of *porphyrins*. Someone with AIP produces these *porphyrins* which act as nerve toxins. Various factors can cause an explosion of porphyrin production which brings on violent attacks."

"Barbiturates *can* actually induce, bring on, porphyria attacks?"

"Yes. If I remember correctly, no one really understands the mechanism. But barbiturates are definitely a danger to someone with AIP." Suddenly Daniel clapped his forehead. "Oh, Jesus, I think I just remembered something! The para-

medics gave her phenytoin sodium . . . Dilantin
. . . for the seizure. That's standard procedure,
but Dilantin is also a drug that induces porphyria
attacks."

"If someone gave Magda the barbiturates," Delia said slowly, "knowing she had acute intermittent porphyria . . . ?"

"It would be murder," Daniel said with finality
in his voice. "It's a quirky disease, but one thing
is sure. Barbiturates, even in small doses, can
cause an acute, devastating—and potentially fa-
tal—attack."

"We know the Seconal was administered," Delia said, "over a period of months in small
doses—the daily dose of her supposed birth control pills." She paused. "By the way, I found the
man who made up that 'prescription.' " Daniel's
eyes widened. "During my night out on the town,
I was meeting with a drug dealer who will do
anything—no questions asked—for the right
price."

Delia saw the twofold impact of this information register on her lover. Then he said, "Did he
tell you who placed this special order?"

"No," Delia said and decided for reasons she
did not entirely fathom at this point to keep the
details of her conversation with Dr. Don to herself for now. "No, he just said he made up the
order some time in the last year."

"Who could have switched the pills?"

"Oh, it's the same list—Charlotte, Ned, Jason." Suddenly a thought struck Delia. "Perhaps

also . . ." she murmured as an image of hard angry faces crossed her vision.

"Perhaps?"

"Nothing—a thought I'll follow up on."

Daniel rubbed at his chin with his hand. "It would be real nice to get more information on AIP. Might give us some ideas. I could do a library search, but it will take some time to get the stuff. The wheels of government grind really slow when you need something fast."

"Would a university library have all the necessary journals?"

"Yes," Daniel said, "if there's a medical school."

"I could go up to Boston and use the Harvard Library. I still have connections there."

"Ah . . . leave it to Viscountess Ross-Merlani to have all the right friends in the right places."

Delia stiffened. "In this case, it's Professor Ross-Merlani."

"Pardon, Professor. I didn't see you change your ermine robe for academic gown. As usual it happened too fast."

"Please, Daniel," Delia said in a gentle voice, "not now, not tonight." She stroked his face.

"Yes—all right. I'm sorry." But the mood of intimacy between them was briefly broken once again. And as Daniel took her in his arms, Delia wondered how many more times they could apply a patch.

Hours later, the moisture of Daniel's kisses still

upon her mouth, Delia lay awake, thinking. Finally, she slipped from his embrace and placed a phone call to Western Union International. She gave instructions for a wire to be sent to Signor Federico Merlani and dictated a message in Italian.

Papa,
   I know how thorough you are and how you like each detail in place. So I have decided to simplify the matter of my thirtieth birthday present. Although the occasion is still several months hence, I would like my present now, if you please. I need a car, Papa, to drive myself. I do hate so to shop, and this is the sort of thing you know so well. I'm at the Carlyle. I am fine—saw Adela—she looked lovely. Hope all is well with you.
Your loving daughter,
Giulietta

Chapter Twenty-four

On the Trail

When Daniel Elliot and Delia Ross-Merlani emerged from the Carlyle Hotel on a bright, sunny morning several days after their reunion, they were greeted by a sight other than the usual rush hour traffic. Signor Paolo Conti, senior vice-president of Ferrari Motors North America, was waiting for them, standing in front of a silver Ferrari 348ts.

"Lady Delia—how nice to see you again."

"Buon giorno, Signor Conti. Permit me to present my friend, Dr. Elliot." The two gentlemen shook hands.

"Your father asked me to personally see to your birthday gift. May I join him in wishing you *Buon Compleanno."*

"Thank you," she said, holding out her hand for the keys. He gave them to her, kissed her hand and then bade the couple farewell.

"Today's your birthday?"

"Oh, no—it's in November—November twenty-seventh. I just needed a car. So I wired Papa to make me a little present."

"A little present?"

She shrugged. "It means nothing to him. Papa owns a packet of Ferrari stock." She looked at the sleek automobile and smiled. "I will say, however, that sometimes my father is capable of surprising me."

"Surprising you—how so? You knew he was sending a car."

"Oh, yes," Delia said. "But his choice of model is rather touching in its own way. Papa simply has most things handled by a series of sycophants. But in this case, the gift has the unmistakable marks of his own effort. He clearly ordered this car for me himself, and that is rare."

"How do you know that?" Daniel asked.

"Well, had one of his minions done it—I think we would be looking at the Ferrari F40. It's a rather garish, futuristic car—only a limited number were made, and it's the sort of thing that will turn heads in the street. It also costs about four times what most Ferraris cost. Since this is not the most expensive, nor the most flashy—which would have been the obvious choice of one of his underlings who would have assumed my father would only want the top of the line—Papa must have ordered this one specifically for me."

For a moment, the couple stood looking at this sleek, gleaming object catching the light amid the come and go of a busy Madison Avenue morning. Then Delia smiled. "I think I just got it . . . why he chose this one. When I was a little girl, I often spent Christmas with my father. He would usually read to me from a children's book which his mother used to read to him each Christmas. It was a fairy tale—*La Carrozza d'Argento*—*The Silver Carriage*. It was about a princess who must wait for the arrival of her prince in the shining silver carriage. I guess my father must have remembered that story and ordered this one for me."

Daniel saw something of the wistfulness in his lover's smile, and softly he said, "And given that, you feel better about his gift to you? As if it now has some context, some meaning?"

Delia turned steely eyes upon him. "As far as Adela and Papa are concerned, I take what I can get." The look on her face indicated that the subject was now closed.

Mrs. MacPhee appeared carrying a small suitcase. She eyed the car. "How very nice," she said. Delia opened the trunk, and Mrs. MacPhee stowed the bag. "Have a safe trip, Miss Delia."

Delia bent down and kissed Mrs. MacPhee's cheek. "Thank you, darling. You and the mister enjoy your holiday. I'll be back in a couple of days—I'll call and let you know just when."

"Drive carefully!" Mrs. MacPhee commanded in parting.

"May I drop you at the office?" Delia asked her lover.

"No," Daniel said, "I have a meeting at Gracie

Mansion—I'll hop a cab. What time do you have to meet Charlotte?"

"Ten minutes ago," Delia said with a smile.

Daniel took her in his arms and kissed her. "Have a good trip and see that you heed Mrs. Mac's advice."

"I'll call you tonight and let you know the lay of the land."

Daniel nuzzled her neck, and said, "I already know the lay of the land." Delia poked him, then kissed him goodbye.

Daniel got into a cab as Delia got behind the wheel of her car. She briefly let her gaze rest upon the expected green-flowered bottle with her father's card attached. Admiring the sleek beauty and design of her new possession, she turned the key in the ignition and raced the engine for a long time. The surge of power seemed to keep pace with the blood coursing through her veins. A smile of satisfaction filled her wide mouth then as she put the car and her investigation into gear.

Charlotte Maitland remained silent for some time after the initial discussion of the new car. Delia cast side-long glances at her friend, but was unable to read her countenance.

Finally Charlotte broke the silence and said, "This was a good idea. I think I need to get away."

Delia shifted into fourth and said, "You've

been a busy lass lately. Always gadding about."

Charlotte shrugged. "I'm trying not to think."

"Think or feel, Charley?"

Charlotte sighed. "Feel, I suppose. Things just seem to be happening too fast — at least for me."

"Not just Mags's murder?"

Charlotte looked at her friend. "Then, it *was* definitely murder?"

Delia nodded. "I don't have it all yet. Do you want to know?"

"Yes," Charlotte said, her face gone quite pale.

"You're to discuss this with *no one,*" Delia said.

Charlotte's head gave a brief bob.

"Magda apparently suffered from a rare genetic disorder called acute intermittent porphyria. It causes violent episodic gastric attacks and, in its worst manifestations, seizures. The attacks are usually precipitated by chemical changes in the body. Menstruation might cause an attack, as might an infection and some medications. Barbiturates definitely induce attacks."

"But how can that have been, Delia? Magda was ill for years and was in and out of hospital. The doctors ran so many, many tests."

"It's a very rare disease, Charley, and the symptoms seem like so many other things. It often goes undiagnosed for many years. Unless there is a known family history."

"So no one knew?"

Delia paused. "Someone did know. Someone must have figured it out and switched Mags's birth control pills to Seconals some time in the last year. I have ascertained that someone did switch her pills—that what Mags thought were her birth control pills actually contained Seconal. That's why she had more and more episodes this last year. Eventually one of the attacks killed her."

"But who?" Charlotte asked, her voice sharp.

"I don't know that yet, not for certain. Besides yourself, who else had access to Magda's pills since the attacks became more regular?"

"Well, Ned of course and . . . Jason, I guess." Charlotte's voice faltered.

Delia looked quickly at her friend. "Charley . . . I don't . . . want to. . . ."

"It's all right, Delia. I'm not in love with him. But I like being with him. He's so sweet—like a little boy."

"And you like that quality?"

"I don't know what I like. You see . . . there's also Pete. We've gone out several times," Charlotte said simply. Delia remained silent but thought, "Ah, 'Urban Sociology' explained."

"In some ways Pete is like a little boy, too," Charlotte continued. "Very rough and tumble—but he can also be very gentle."

"Are you falling in love with him?"

"I don't know."

"Have you . . . ?"

Charlotte colored a bit. "I've thought about it . . . about how I would feel making love with each of them. I'm obviously unsure of my feel-

214

ings so. . . ."

"Just take it easy, Charley. Listen to your heart. It won't steer you wrong. When you're sure of your feelings, you'll know what to do. And any man who really cares for you will understand and appreciate you."

"Are you in love with Daniel?" Charlotte asked.

Delia frowned, decided to pass the two cars in front of her, accelerated to ninety-seven—cursing the American laws that prevented one from driving at the truly sensible three-digit speeds of European highways—and executed the maneuver. She felt better afterward and said, "I don't know about that either."

For a moment, Delia's hand left the stick shift and held her friend's. Their eyes, however, remained on the long stretch of road ahead, seeming to search out some final destination each now imagined must lay in the distance.

Chapter Twenty-five

Tea Time

"What did you do today?" The two women were seated the following evening in their suite at the Ritz having dinner.

Charlotte wiped her fingers carefully on a linen napkin and said, "I went to the Isabella Stewart Gardner Museum. I hadn't been there since . . . since Magda lived in Cambridge years ago."

"It's ever so lovely a place," Delia said, pouring some more champagne into their glasses.

Charlotte nodded. "Today there was a group of school children — black children mostly — with their teacher. They were so sweet. And very excited by what they saw." Charlotte's face went from wistful to serious. "I've been thinking, Delia, of taking a job next September. Teaching, again. I've been thinking about it for some time, and Pete knows a woman who runs a day-care center for ghetto children. I thought . . . perhaps. . . ."

Delia took her friend's hand and gave it a gentle squeeze. "Sounds grand, Charley. Just the ticket. You were very happy teaching, as I remember."

"Yes," Charlotte said, "I love little ones." She paused and asked hesitantly, "What did you do today?"

"Had lunch with Professor Donnelly over at Harvard. Wonderful old gent, hasn't changed a jot. Then he went with me to the library—pulled some strings and arranged for a computer search on porphyria. That's the next lead to follow. Should have a packet of stuff for me to look at sometime tomorrow—in the late afternoon."

"Well, what shall we do tomorrow?"

"I was thinking, Charley. Let's pay a call on Mrs. Hennessey."

Charlotte looked up in surprise. "Whatever for?"

Delia fingered her hair for a moment. "Didn't Patrick *et sa mère* stay with Magda and Ned at their house in Whitinsville last summer? Just before Magda moved out with Jason?"

"Yes . . . and it was a horrid time, Magda said. They'd all been there for Easter before that . . . and there'd been that dreadful scene . . . you remember, I told you. Patrick had tried to make love to Magda—oh, he was drunk, I suspect— and Mrs. Hennessey had called Magda such awful names. Said Magda was destroying both of her sons . . . that she was 'unfit to breathe the same air as they did!' Oh, very awful. So the

217

gathering last summer was to try and heal the wounds."

"And?"

"Magda said everyone was very polite and that it made her 'positively nauseous.' She left Ned a week after they returned to New York," Charlotte said.

"Oh, yes. Then we should definitely pay a visit *chez* Hennessey. They will see you, won't they?"

"I believe so. Mrs. Hennessey always liked me. But, Delia, I don't quite see the point."

"Perhaps there isn't one, Charley. But during that visit to Whitinsville, Patrick and Mother Hennessey had access to Magda's pills. And both indeed had a motive. Oh, one other thing—can you remember any time between Easter and the summer visit that Patrick made a trip to New York?"

Charlotte thought for a moment and then nodded. "Yes—last June after school ended. Patrick stayed at Ned and Magda's for about a week to discuss family matters. I remember because Magda wanted so very much to get out of their apartment. We flew to London for a couple of weeks—stayed at your flat. You remember—you were in Italy."

"Yes, Papa's 'royal summons' to meet his latest—Madame Mala."

"That visit to London was the last trip Mags and I ever took together." Charlotte's voice broke just a little.

"Well, we must talk to Patrick, then. Think you can handle it? Might get nasty."

"Yes . . . yes, I'm sure I can."

"Good. Ring up Mrs. Hennessey and arrange it."

"Delia, do you think . . . ?"

"Thinking is all I can do, Charlotte. For now."

The Hennessey home was a small, square, neat house on Somerset Street. Mrs. Hennessey, somewhat stiff, motioned the two women in. Patrick sat in the living room, pouring tea. He rose to greet them.

"I'm glad to see you, Charlotte."

"You remember my friend Delia Ross-Merlani." Everyone murmured appropriate but cool greetings.

"Are you on holiday?" Delia inquired politely of Patrick.

"Holiday? . . . oh, vacation . . . yes, school's out for the year."

"Are you a history instructor like your brother?" Delia asked, her voice having taken on that sweet ingenue-like quality that she had found so helpful in the process of interrogation. She made a mental note to ask Detective Pete if he had ever considered cultivating such a manner.

"No, I teach biology and chemistry at a Catholic high school for boys here in our parish."

"Ah, the scientist in the family," Delia said

with her brightest smile.

"How are you getting on, Charlotte?" Mrs. Hennessey asked.

"I'm all right. Over the shock at least. I haven't spoken to Ned in a while . . . is . . . he . . . is he . . . ?"

Mrs. Hennessey's face looked suddenly to Delia like one of those grim masks from early Greek tragedy. "He's fine . . . much better now, in fact." She stressed the word "now."

"Mother," Patrick said soothingly.

"Don't 'Mother' me, Patrick. For years I held my tongue, and for years everyone suffered. I'm sorry for your loss, Charlotte. I would not wish *you* harm, but I'm glad your sister's dead. And if there is truly divine retribution, then she's burning in the fires of Hell for what she did to my sons!"

Charlotte began to speak, but Delia placed a restraining hand on her arm. This scene, like something out of a bad O'Neill drama, interested her immensely. But seeing the need to remove at least the reminder of an outsider's presence, Delia turned her glance casually away, seeming to study some books on a shelf.

"Please don't upset yourself, Mother," Patrick said, his voice pleading now.

"No," Mrs. Hennessey said, "oh, no. That wicked, wicked she-devil wasn't content with just one of my boys. Oh, no! Just look at him!" She pointed an accusatory finger at Patrick. "First he lusts after his brother's wife, and now he's consumed with tears for her."

"That's not so," Patrick shouted suddenly and jumped to his feet. His face was twisted in pain. "I hated her, hated her every moment."

"Hated her?!" Mrs. Hennessey spit out the words.

"Yes, we . . . we used to sit there, day after day, together at Whitinsville. Her eyes were so blue, so bright." He turned to Charlotte and said in a small voice, "I thought she liked me, was interested in me. When I talked with her, she seemed so kind, so beautiful. I told her . . . told her things . . . about how I felt. No one had ever listened before as she did."

"I'm sure she did like you," Charlotte said quietly.

But heedless now of the others, Patrick's eyes stared ahead to some vision only he could see. "One time when I came to New York, we went out together, just the two of us, to this dancing club. I didn't know how to dance, but Magda didn't care. She just laughed and laughed and showed me how to move to the music. And I did learn—I did! And it was fun," he said, and his voice suddenly broke.

Patrick began to weep then, weeping as a child might. "And then one day in Whitinsville, she came to my room to say good night. She looked like an angel. She bent down to kiss me, and she seemed so sad. I think she was very unhappy. No

221

one really loved her, you see. Not really. And I could smell her then — her warmth — like flowers. And *I* . . . I . . . loved her. Oh, Sweet Jesus, I loved her! Then she said, 'Oh, Patty, you are such a silly boy.'

"Well, I'm not a silly boy!" Patrick suddenly began to shout at the unseen presence all felt. "I'm a man — a grown man! And I wanted her then as a man would. I began to touch her . . . to make love to her . . . and then she hit me . . . she struck me hard across the face." Patrick's hand went up to his cheek. "I could . . . could taste the blood in my mouth. And then I wanted to hurt her, too! I grabbed her and began to shake her and shake her and. . . ." Patrick collapsed then, the sobs now shaking his big frame.

Mrs. Hennessey rose quietly and went to her son. She cradled his head against her breasts and murmured soothingly, "There, there, my boy. It's all right now. Mother's here."

Delia and Charlotte exchanged a look, stood up, and silently prepared to take their leave. At the door, Charlotte said softly, "I'm sorry, Mrs. Hennessey — I'm sorry for many things." Mrs. Hennessey turned her face to them; her look of righteous hatred was the only reply.

Outside, Delia and her friend stood for a moment to let the summer's sun take away the chill in their bones. "What do you think really happened?" Delia asked as they walked to her car.

Charlotte shrugged. "I don't know, Delia.

Probably Magda did feel sorry for Patrick and was kind to him. He mistook the signs. Magda liked to play her games with men—but surely not with the likes of Patrick."

"In some ways, though," Delia said carefully, "he's like Jason. Childlike, sweet. They even look alike—tall, broad-shouldered."

"Yes," Charlotte agreed, "I guess that's so. But for that matter, Ned is tall and broad-shouldered, too. And I can see a way in which he must have once had a kind of childlike quality to him. He was desperately in love with Magda when he first met her. Bombarded her with notes and nosegays and whatever other romantic notions he could think of. I think, perhaps, it is big men who are really only grown-up children that are attracted to women like Magda—because such women are fragile and angelic-looking."

"Tell me, Charlotte," Delia said thoughtfully, "as a matter of supposition—do you think Patrick would do anything his mother asked?"

Charlotte's brown eyes registered the significance of this question. "No," she said slowly. "But, Delia, do you remember those lines of Peele's—Magda quoted them once to us in speaking about Patrick. We were having tea at Claridge's."

Delia searched through her memories and finally came upon that moment from their shared past. "Yes, I think I do. 'Beauty, strength, youth are flowers, but fading seen;/ Duty, faith, love, are roots, and ever green.' I see what you mean, Charley. Magda was like flowers to Patrick. And his mother his roots."

"I don't know that Patrick would do anything his mother asked. But I do think he would have done a great deal to make up for his fall from grace."

Delia put an arm round her friend. *"Mia cara,* sometimes you are wise beyond your years. Come on, let's get us some wine to wash the taste of tea and ash from our mouths."

Chapter Twenty-six

A King's Ransom

"Are you sure you're up to driving?"

"Oh, yes," Delia said breezily.

"But you were reading so late into the night . . . I thought. . . ."

"Yes, I was looking through the stack of materials from the Harvard Library. There's quite a lot."

"Did you . . . did you learn anything?"

Delia glanced at her friend. "I'm not hiding anything from you, Charley. Whatever you want to know, ask. I only have a few pieces of the puzzle thus far."

"I know, Delia. I trust you absolutely."

Delia gave her a smile and then said, "Charley, tell me again about Mags's will. She left her jewelry to you . . . and the rest of her estate?"

"It was divided equally between Ned and myself."

"Nothing for Jason?"

"No. The will was made shortly after Magda's marriage."

"And she didn't change it or update it?"

"No. She said she was going to. I thought she had, as a matter of fact. But you know . . . Magda was never really very reliable about such things. She had the best intentions, no matter what her actions."

"Do you think she meant to stay with Jason . . . that she was really in love with him?"

Charlotte's face grew sad. "I still don't know that, but I like to think so . . . that she found a love that made her happy. But I don't know."

Delia was not surprised to feel tears stinging her own eyes. "Yes," she said quietly, "I like to think that, too."

"It seems rather dreadful, really. Magda being ill and someone using that to kill her."

"Yes, it is dreadful. Perhaps more dreadful than we suppose," Delia murmured. "To knowingly watch someone die like that."

"You were reading about her disease last night?"

"Not really reading. The articles are mostly from medical journals—far too technical for me. Daniel will have to have a go at them."

The two women lapsed into silence again. But Charlotte noticed that there was still a frown in the corner of her friend's eyes. Something, she knew, was on Delia's mind.

At the turnoff onto Route 91, Delia said softly, *"Oh, merde, mon amie.* Charlotte, do you know which particular period is Ned's specialty?"

"Yes, eighteenth century—the Hanoverians, I believe."

"Yes, that's what I just remembered. Do you recall the particular subject of his doctoral dissertation?"

"No, I don't."

"Ay, minchione, I saw a copy of it yesterday on the bookshelf above the desk at Mother Hennessey's: 'George III and John Wilkes: Mistaken Motives.' "

"Oh, yes, that's right. I do recall it now. Magda sent me a copy."

"Do you have it still?"

"Somewhere, I'm sure. Why?"

Delia quickly pulled over to the side of the road, and turned to her friend. "While the library was doing the computer search, I looked through some books on my own. And I learned that scientists now believe that the reason ole King George III became potty was that he suffered from an obscure disease called porphyria. It's been buzzing in my head all day," Delia said. "King George—porphyria . . ."

". . . Ned," Charlotte said, her voice hollow.

Delia caught Charlotte's tone. "Careful, Charley, careful. Don't jump to any hasty conclusions. You have a copy of Ned's dissertation if it comes

227

to that."

"Yes," Charlotte said, "and so do Patrick and Mrs. Hennessey. They all hated Magda—all of the Hennesseys—they all might have tormented and killed my sister."

"I imagine that's so," Delia said thoughtfully. "Even Ned must have hated her enough to kill her."

"I must know, Delia. I must know who did this terrible thing to my sister. *We* must know."

"Yes, Charlotte. This is another thing you and I must find out. For ourselves. . . ." Delia's face softened, and she hugged Charlotte to her. And each woman read the thought clearly in the other's heart, "For Magdalene."

Chapter Twenty-seven

Packaging

Delia felt Daniel's presence in the room and unhurriedly finished Royer's *La Sensible*. Then she closed the harpsichord and turned to face him.

"My eyes are almost purple from reading those articles," Daniel said with his boyish grin.

Delia shook her head like a school mistress. "And?"

"And I would say it's absolutely likely that Magdalene Maitland Hennessey had acute intermittent porphyria and person or persons unknown bumped her off."

Delia nodded. "The only thing that still puzzles me, Daniel, is why Magda had no attacks during all her years of the *high* life. I know for a fact that she took many colorful drugs including 'reds' and other barbiturates."

"Actually, according to the literature I've read, it's not all that surprising that Magda was symptom-free for so long. Apparently the disease is latent throughout most of childhood and generally well into the patient's twenties. That's another reason it's so hard to diagnose. Drugs that were seemingly safe for Magda at twenty-one killed her at thirty-one." Daniel paused for a moment rubbing his jaw and said thoughtfully, "Which someone obviously knew."

"Dr. Don described the purchaser of the pills as a big, red-bearded chap," Delia said slowly.

Daniel absorbed this piece of information. "Well, Ned seems to have had ample reason to kill Magda. Her obvious charms aside, a man might say 'enough is enough.' "

"Might a man say that?" Delia asked pointedly.

"Some men might," Daniel said, returning her gaze. "No matter how much in love one is with a woman, there are always limits."

"How does a woman find out those limits?"

"Only by testing them, I think," Daniel said. He watched Delia as she took in his gentle reproof and then went on. "Is Ned's half of the estate a sizable chunk?"

"Oh, yes—tied up in stocks most of it—about six hundred thousand pounds, Charley said."

Daniel whistled. "Wow. His share's more than a million bucks. And he must have known about porphyria."

"Yes," Delia said, "I read through Charlotte's copy of his dissertation. He cites several articles on the king's disease when he discusses George's madness and its effect on his policies."

"The pieces fit rather neatly," Daniel observed.

"It's not the only one that's neat. Patrick is a science teacher and naturally would understand all about porphyria. I'm sure that he not only read Ned's dissertation, but likely helped Ned during his research in understanding all about the disease. And Patrick had not only an opportunity to make a switch in the pills, but he also had an opportunity to meet the dealer who prepared them. His kind of passionate love-hate for Magda, mixed with his guilt, could have driven him to murder. Charley feels that Patrick would have done almost anything to regain his mother's love. And Mama Hennessey certainly wanted Magda dead."

"Yes," Daniel agreed, "that's also rather neat."

"Then again, Magda's copy of the dissertation was at Jason's. Maybe he read it. Thought it might help him to understand something about Ned and therefore more about Magda. Maybe he realized that Magda had porphyria and killed her," Delia said.

"Why would Jason kill Magda? He certainly

seemed in love with her."

"Well, from much of what Charley remembers, Magda talked about a permanent future with Jason. Magda had told Charlotte that she intended to change her will. I imagine she assured Jason of the same thing. But she was . . . in current parlance . . . a bit flaky about such things. Jason's a sweet boy, but not much of an actor. I asked around at the Saturnalia—he had lots of debts before Magdalene entered his life. Since it took a number of months to kill Magda, Jason had a chance to really cement their relationship. The more ill she became, the more she clung to him. He might have killed her thinking he, and not Ned, was going to get her money."

"Perhaps," Daniel said, "Jason didn't intend to kill her. Just keep her sick enough to keep her dependent on him."

Delia frowned. "Or Ned might have hypothesized that illness would drive Magda back to him."

"That's also rather neat," Daniel commented dryly.

"I mistrust these tidy little parcels as much as I do loose ends. Something, I think, is wrong. It's such a dreadful crime when you think of it. Someone actually watched Magda in agony and let her suffer over and over until she died."

"Well, in that case, I should think that whoever killed her must have hated her very much," Daniel said.

Delia slowly shook her head, and a strange expression came over her features. "Perhaps, though . . . ," she murmured.

Daniel opened his mouth to ask a question and then changed his mind at the look on her face. He had learned quite well that Delia would keep her own counsel till she was ready to speak.

It was the phone's ringing that woke Delia up, and she listened as Daniel spoke quietly into it. Then he said, "Delia, it's Charlotte. She seems very upset and wants to talk to you."

Delia cast a swift glance at the clock beside the bed: 5:41. She was instantly awake. "Yes, Charley."

"I'm sorry," Charlotte said in a hoarse voice, "but I've been ever so ill all night."

"Ill?"

"Yes. I have terrible cramps and a high fever. I've been vomiting for hours."

Delia felt herself go cold with fear. She turned to Daniel and said, "Charley's ill. Vomiting and cramps."

He took the phone from her. "Charlotte, just

relax. We'll pick you up in about ten minutes. Have you taken anything?"

"Just some bicarb. It didn't stay down."

"Okay. Don't eat or drink anything at all. Delia and I will come and get you." He pushed down the button to place another call. "I'll get Helen Friedman — an old friend and top GI specialist. She'll admit Charlotte to the hospital for tests."

"Daniel, can it be AIP?"

"Oh, yes, Delia. Porphyria is an inherited disease, and Charlotte could have it."

"But what might have brought it on now?"

"A minor infection, perhaps. Or menstruation. It just might be beginning for Charlotte as it finally began for Magda."

"But it also finally ended Magda. Can you do anything or . . . ?" The fear in Delia's voice was palpable.

Daniel took her shaking body into his arms. "We can give her some medication for the vomiting and an IV to prevent her from dehydrating. That can help. And we'll watch her very carefully."

Delia nodded and quickly began to dress. But in spite of the muggy July morning and Daniel's arm about her as she left his apartment, she still felt terribly, terribly cold.

* * *

"I don't remember much after I got here."

Delia held Charlotte's hand tightly in her own. She was relieved to see some of the natural blush back in her friend's cheeks. "Well, Dr. Friedman examined you and then took some X-rays. They ruled out a bleeding ulcer and appendicitis. And she ordered a high carbohydrate infusion. That would help if it's porphyria," she said softly.

"Do I have it?" Charlotte asked, clutching Delia's hand.

"The tests aren't finished yet. You did have a high white count and some of the symptoms—pain, vomiting."

"I slept most of yesterday, didn't I?"

Delia nodded. "That was the pain medication."

"If I . . . I . . . have it . . . what does that mean?"

"It means you have to be careful about certain drugs, treat any infection immediately and . . . just be aware of the symptoms. Many people who have it live long, productive lives."

"Will I be able to have children?" Charlotte asked quietly.

Delia shut her eyes for a second and thought, "Oh, *foutre!*" Then to her friend, she said, "I don't know, Charley." There was a tap on the door, and Daniel came in with Dr. Friedman.

"How are you feeling, Charlotte?" Dr. Friedman asked.

"A bit dizzy, but better."

"Fine."

"There's good news," Daniel said smiling, "and some baddish news. Which do you want?"

"The good," Charlotte said, sounding to Delia's ears like a meek child before the headmistress.

"You don't have acute intermittent porphyria," Dr. Friedman said. Charlotte began to cry then, groping for a tissue. Delia got two out of her bag, one for her own streaming eyes.

"And the baddish?" Delia said after a moment.

"You had quite a bout of salmonella."

"Salmonella?"

"Commonly called food poisoning. Can you remember what you ate before you got sick?" Dr. Friedman asked.

Charlotte frowned. "Well, when we got back from Boston, I had little in the house. So I went out to the market . . . and . . . and—" She stopped. "Oh, dear," she said.

"Oh, dear, what?" Delia asked, her eyes narrowed.

"Well, there was this woman, a vendor with a cart, selling souvlaki. And she had this sweet, sweet little boy with her. Dark eyes and dark curls, oh, Delia, he would've made your heart melt. I smiled at him and we began to chat. I didn't think there was anything wrong . . . I bought one of the sandwiches. It was a bit on the greasy side, but I so liked the little boy."

"Well, that certainly could do it. Those vendors are notorious for having tainted meat," Daniel said.

Delia smiled fondly at her friend. "Leave it to Charlotte to get food poisoning because of a little child's eyes. What happens now?"

"I think you should stay another day or so, Charlotte. You were quite weakened when we admitted you, and I would like to get some antibiotics into you through the IV. You can go home when you're stronger," Dr. Friedman concluded.

Charlotte gave a small but happy smile and nodded. Delia said, "I'll stay with her for several days when she gets home." Dr. Friedman said she'd look in the next day and then left. Charlotte lay back on her pillows and heaved a deep sigh. "Amen," Delia said.

"You look more wiped out than she does," Daniel said, looking at Delia.

"Yes, Delia. You should go home and rest. You've been here for two whole days."

"I'm fine," Delia said imperviously.

"You'll be no help to Charlotte unless you're rested," Daniel replied.

Delia opened her mouth to retort but yawned instead. Daniel and Charlotte looked at her pointedly. "Caught red-handed," she murmured.

Just then the phone rang. Delia answered. "Oh, hello, Pete . . . yes, she's fine . . . a visit?" Charlotte nodded. "Yes, that would be lovely. *Sì, Sì. Non abbiate paura! Va bene. Sì, ciao.*" She replaced the receiver. "That's one very concerned *bambino.*"

The phone rang again. Delia reached for it and said, "And that's another, I imagine. Let me handle this. Hello? . . . oh, hello, Jason. Yes . . . much better . . . on the mend. No . . . a bit of stomach trouble. Might be a touch of a bug or a bit of bad food . . . that's all . . . a visit? Perhaps when she's home. Yes . . . I'll ring you up. Righty-o. Bye."

"Why did you say — ?" Charlotte began, but was interrupted by the appearance of Mrs. MacPhee.

"Well, my gel," she said, "how are you getting on?"

"Much better, Mrs. Mac."

Mrs. MacPhee sat down beside Charlotte, removed some knitting that would have been the envy of Madame DeFarge, and fixed a baleful eye on her mistress. "The car is waiting downstairs, Miss Delia. You go straightaway to the hotel and to bed. I'll sit with Miss Charlotte."

Again Delia opened her mouth to protest,

238

but surrendered at the sight of the determined faces all around her. "Yes, ma'am."

"I'll see you to the car," Daniel said. Delia kissed Charlotte goodbye with promises of her return that evening.

"Oh, Miss Delia . . . Professor Hennessey called," Mrs. MacPhee said.

Delia wheeled round from the doorway. "Oh?"

"Said he'd heard you'd been visiting with his mother. Sounded a bit miffy, I thought. I told him you were at hospital with Miss Charlotte who was ill. That took him down a peg or two."

"Then what did he say?"

"Oh, he asked a number of questions about Miss Charlotte. What was wrong? Had it come on sudden like? What hospital . . . ?"

"What did you tell him?"

"That she was taken poorly two nights ago with a stomach sickness."

"That's all?"

"Why, yes," Mrs. MacPhee said in surprise. "What more is there to tell?"

Delia looked at Charlotte. "Nothing more. Nothing at all to anyone. 'Taken poorly with a stomach sickness.' " Charlotte nodded.

As they waited for the elevator, Daniel said, "What are you up to?"

"I'm not sure yet. But I might be able to

make my own neat little parcel." In the elevator, she began to kiss Daniel, but it turned into a great, sweet yawn.

Chapter Twenty-eight

On the Run

As Delia turned the key to open Charlotte Maitland's front door, she had the immediate sense of an occupied space. Although it was dark inside and she heard no sound, she felt the absolute presence of another person. Calmly, she sang out, "Char-ley."

Delia knew full well that her friend was still in the hospital, having just left her less than an hour before. Indeed, she had come over to get some additional clean clothes for Charlotte. Instead now, Delia noisily went into the kitchen and rummaged about. Then she left the apartment, locking the door behind her.

Delia got into the elevator, rode to the first floor and waited. The elevator began to move again, and she took one trip up to the fourteenth floor, where an elderly couple got in, and Delia rode down with them. At the second floor, her ladyship went through an elaborate pantomime as if she'd forgotten something. The couple emerged at the ground floor, and with a smile, Delia remained in the elevator as the doors closed.

In another minute, the elevator ascended again, this time to the eleventh floor. As the elevator doors opened Delia said, "Good afternoon."

For only a fraction of a second, she caught sight of the retreating back of a tall red-bearded man as he turned and fled quickly down the stairs. Once again Delia let herself into Charlotte's apartment and now got the items she had originally come for. Then she took a brief tour of the apartment, paying particular attention to the places where Charlotte had put her late sister's belongings. Finally, with a smile of satisfaction, she turned out the lights and locked up once again.

Pocketing the keys to Charlotte's apartment, Delia began to sing in her thin, not particularly pleasant voice, lines from her favorite Gilbert and Sullivan aria: " 'Never mind the why and wherefore, love can level ranks and therefore. . . .' " Suddenly Delia broke into a happy, high laugh at the inadvertent appropriateness of her selection.

"I think he's really falling in love with her," Daniel said as he traced a line down Delia's back with his hand.

Delia considered this. "In many ways, they're an odd couple."

"Odd for him, especially," Daniel agreed. "I mean, Pete's from the old 'Slam-bam-thank-you-ma'am' school of relationships."

"What about Linda?"

Daniel's face clouded over. "Yes. That was different. First time either one of them ever fell in love, and there was so much pain."

"I gather not only for them."

"No," Daniel said. "Pete's family and mine were really upset. It was hard for Pete and Linda—especially as they were so young—to sustain a relationship that made so many people miserable. Linda headed out west, and Pete dived into his work with a vengeance. I think they both found running away easier."

Delia reached out a hand and stroked the side of her lover's face. "And you, can you sustain a relationship that makes others unhappy?"

Daniel turned over to face the woman at his side. "It's not the same thing. Besides, I'm not the type to run away, Delia."

She thought this over. "No, you won't run," she said, still gently stroking his face and gazing into his eyes. Then she thought, "Not like me."

As if reading her mind Daniel said, "In this way, my darling, I truly don't run to type. I'm not seeking anyone's approval for what I do with my life."

"Really, Daniel?"

He shook his head. "I don't know yet what I want. But when I do, it will be my own choice,

243

my own decision. And then, you'll be the first to know, Delia."

Delia let this hang in the air between them and finally asked in a low hesitant voice, "Then, why did you take me home to meet your family?"

"I took you home to meet them because I wanted you to learn something of me, my life, my beginnings."

"I genitori," she murmured.

"Yes," he said. "I hoped they would like you, accept you, but that wasn't what was important to me."

"What was?"

"That you see who I am and accept me. That's all."

Delia thought about this for a long moment. They had never discussed that painful night, and she knew now to tread very carefully. "So you thought my supposed condescension to your parents was a snub . . . a rejection of you?" Daniel nodded. "Oh, my Daniel, you are a fool," she said, her voice edged with tears. "If I have learned anything in my tattered little emotional life, it's to respect people for themselves and not for their trappings. God, if someone were to judge me by the Ross clan and Merlani mountebanks, I'd certainly be in big trouble. Oh, no, Daniel, I value you for who you are." She kissed him and felt so grateful for the intensity of his response. "I think I am beginning now to understand how you came to be that person. That's all that matters to us."

"Tunc?" Daniel asked, although there was a hollow like a blade beneath his heart.

Delia floundered, lost her footing and quickly righted herself again. "And . . . I shall be here to see what you become."

Daniel bowed his head in acceptance of this. It was a hedge, a plea for time, he knew, and not quite the answer to his heart's query. But again he recognized that the spirit of this woman could not be acquired, only given freely by her. He looked up at Delia and smiled into her eyes. She smiled back at him, warming for the moment that shaded place where his fear resided.

"Do you think Charlotte is falling in love with Pete?" Daniel asked as they snuggled close together again.

"No, not yet. But she is taking him very seriously, which is a big step for her."

"And what about her feelings for Jason?"

"I don't know. It's a queer business. My guess is she's keeping him in her life as a kind of safeguard against her growing feelings for Pete. She cares for Jason, but I imagine that it's mostly a fraternal feeling."

"How does Jason feel about her?"

"I don't know, but—" Delia's voice was interrupted by the ring of the phone.

She picked it up, listened for a moment, then said, "Fine." To Daniel's look of inquiry she replied, "Telegram on the way up."

Delia put on a Fernando Sanchez dressing gown, answered the door, over-tipped the delivery boy and tore open the envelope. As she read, her face darkened. When she had finished, she tossed the telegram to Daniel, then went into the bathroom and began to run scalding water into the tub.

Sensing danger, Daniel read quickly:

"Delia,
 I want to see you to discuss some urgent business. Please join me as soon as possible.
                    Papa"

Delia returned to the room and picked up the telephone. "What are you going to do?" Daniel asked.

"Call Mrs. Mac—have her make reservations to Milan."

"Have her arrange for two, Delia."

Delia put down the phone and turned to face him. "What?"

"It's summer, I have vacation time—we'll take a trip. You can show me Italy," he said brightly.

"It's summer, brutally hot in Italy, and you have already made the grand tour, after college, I believe you told me."

"Well . . . yes. But I'm sure there are nooks and crannies you could show me. Genova or Cortina, the Dolomites," he ran on enthusiastically.

"Why?" Delia asked.

Daniel's face became serious as he took her two hands in his own. "Because you look unhappy every time the word 'Papa' is mentioned. I'll be with you; maybe it will hurt less because I love you more." Daniel drew her to him. "And I want very much to get away with you. Someplace where we won't think of Magda and murder and mothers for a time. A place where we'll only think of each other. Please, my love." He kissed her, and Delia felt the force of his plea.

She walked to the telephone and once more picked up the receiver. She dialled the MacPhee's suite. "Another holiday for you, *mia cara*. Yes . . . yes, I'm off to Milano . . . a 'summons' from Papa. Yes, tomorrow evening . . . book a flight, *cherie*, for two . . . Daniel and me, please."

Daniel felt his heartbeat quicken as he let out a long drawn breath. And it wasn't until that moment that he realized he had actually been holding it.

Chapter Twenty-nine

Guests

"What's the program?" Daniel asked as they fastened their seat belts for landing at Milan's Malpensa Airport.

"Mrs. Mac wired ahead to Papa's personal secretary. He'll have a car waiting for us. We'll check into the Excelsior Gallia and I'll call Papa."

"Then?"

"Then, depending on how long it takes to finish my business with him, we can drive up through the Alps to Merano and on to Cortina."

"Sounds wonderful—at least the second part."

Outside of Customs, they were met by her father's secretary, Alessandro Balzotti. *"Benvenuto,* Lady Delia."

"Hello, Alessandro. This is Dr. Elliot."

"Hello, Dr. Elliot. Welcome to Milan. Please let me know whatever I may do to help you enjoy your stay."

The chauffeur opened the door of the Rolls

Royce, and the couple sank into the cool, plush seats. As they drove out of the airport Delia said in Italian, "Take us to the Excelsior Gallia first. Then on to see Papa."

The young Italian turned a puzzled gaze onto Delia. "But *Vossignoria,* your father isn't in Milan."

"Not in Milan?"

"Why, no. He is at his villa on the lake."

Delia frowned. "How long has he been there?"

"About ten days."

"With whom?"

The young man's face became a polite mask. "With his staff . . . some friends, perhaps."

Delia's fist came down gently on the seat next to her. She fixed her eyes on her father's secretary, and her words came out in staccato bullets. "I said, Alessandro, with whom?"

Alessandro shrugged. "With Mala Parrotto."

Delia's face did not change. "Instruct the driver to take us to the Villa D'Este." Alessandro immediately began to speak in rapid Italian to the chauffeur.

Delia sat back, put her head on Daniel's shoulder and closed her eyes for a moment. "Jet lag?" he asked gently.

She smiled. "Change of program. We're off to Lake Como."

"I see. Why?"

"It appears Papa is there—at his villa—and his latest *minchia* is his guest."

Daniel didn't understand this last but sensed

the pejorative in her tone. "Oh," he said. "How come your father didn't let you know in his telegram that he was out of town?"

"Papa didn't send the telegram. He has people to do things like that for him. This one was a real botched job, though. The wire didn't explain he was in Como, and it addressed me by the wrong name. If I tell that to Papa, he'll have the poor underling flogged."

"What do you mean by the wrong name?"

"Delia. It was addressed to Delia, which is my English name. My father speaks to me in Italian and always calls me by my second name, Giulietta."

"So we are to visit him at the lake?"

"Yes, but I don't want to stay at his villa till I know what this is about. If at all possible, I should like to avoid having to be pleasant to Madame Mala."

They drove on for nearly an hour and then came along the road through the mountains to Lake Como. Set within a private park was the Grand Hotel Villa D'Este. As the chauffeur opened the door, Delia said, "We are Papa's *guests,* Daniel. One of the things I take—remember?" He nodded.

Delia swept in through the magnificent entrance and walked confidently up to the reception desk. Daniel saw the change in her expression and watched as it descended over her whole carriage; she looked at this moment every inch the peeress.

The manager quickly glided up to Delia, kissed her hand and began to speak in Italian. Delia nodded, murmured and signed the register. Daniel heard his name mentioned. At that, the manager turned to Daniel. "It is an honor to welcome you, Dr. Elliot, to the Villa D'Este. Please be so kind as to sign our book." Daniel did so and waited for his next cue. Delia gave some crisp instructions to Alessandro, and then the couple ascended to their suite. Although it was splendid in every detail, the grandeur of the rooms was dwarfed by the view of Lake Como and the mountains surrounding it.

When they were alone at last, Delia stood beside her lover as they gazed out at the dazzling blue water. She put a hesitant hand on his shoulder. When he turned to look at her, she seemed once more the woman he held nightly in his arms. "It will have to be like this," she said. He nodded. "The only way I can fight him is in my full armor. But I don't want you to feel . . ."

". . . compromised?" Daniel said smiling. He held her to him. "No, Delia. I won't be bothered by it. My manhood doesn't depend on my *paying* my own way."

"No, I didn't think it did." Then with an amused look she asked, "What does it depend on?"

Daniel grinned. "It depends mostly on my *having* my own way. With you," he finished as he backed her up against the bed. They fell together with a laugh and kissed each other till sleep came, the laughter still singing in their ears.

When Daniel Elliot awoke several hours later, his eyes were met by the sight of his lover, sitting cross-legged on the bed, brushing her hair and looking bewildered.

Feeling his gaze she smiled. "Have a good sleep?"

"Mmm," Daniel said. "What have you been doing?"

The look of bewilderment returned. "I had the oddest *tête-à-tête* with Papa over the phone."

"Oh?"

"He said he was very pleasantly surprised to hear from me."

Daniel sat up. "Surprised?"

Delia nodded. "Yes, and he would love us to join him for dinner at his villa—day after tomorrow. He's going to Milan for a meeting tonight, but will be back the next day to receive us." She turned and stared hard at her lover. "Daniel, he said he didn't send for me."

"What?"

"He said he's pleased I'm here, but he has no recollection of instructing that a wire be sent."

Daniel frowned. "Well, that explains why he wasn't in Milan."

"And the error in my name. But not where the telegram came from."

"You don't still have the telegram do you, by any chance?"

252

Delia uncharacteristically colored. "Well, yes. I keep all. . . ."

Daniel took her hand. "I understand, Delia." She smiled gratefully. "We'll let Pete have a look at it. Might be a practical joke or. . . ." The couple exchanged glances.

Delia frowned. "Someone," she thought, "went to a good bit of bother to get me out of the way. I wonder whose way I'm in?" Aloud she said, "Perhaps we should go back, Daniel."

Daniel looked crestfallen for just a moment, but then said smoothly, "Whatever you think is best, Delia."

His face had changed only for an instant, but Delia was acutely aware of his feelings. She remembered how pleased he had been at the prospect of this vacation, how anxious he was to get away with her, away from all the tensions and distractions of the past weeks. She asked herself what was important to her at this time and in this place. And then, with an effort, she shook her mind clear of everything but the man in front of her. Delia put her arms about Daniel's neck. "I think we should stay here and luxuriate in the delights of Lake Como. We'll dine with Papa and then perhaps the next day travel on up into the mountains."

"Sounds good." Then Daniel said, his voice pitched low and hoarse in a pretty fair imitation of Pete Manaro, "How's 'bout some chow?"

"Oh, you . . . you . . . American," Delia said with a smile. "At the Villa D'Este one doesn't get *chow.* One dines on quintessential *cibo!*"

Daniel smiled. " 'Lay on MacDuff . . .' "

"MacDuff? I ever catch you with a MacDuff or MacNair or MacWhatever, I'll—"

Daniel put a gentle hand upon her mouth, pulled her down to him and finished the quotation in her ear, " 'And damn'd be him that first cries, "Hold enough." ' "

Chapter Thirty

Under the Sun

"What time do we dine with your father?"

Delia lifted her head from the cushion and squinted at her lover. " 'Bout eight. Getting bored?"

Daniel looked at the scene before him. They were stretched out side-by-side on lounge chairs round the pool of the Villa D'Este. The gentle motion of the lake rocked the beautiful pool, which like a delicate bubble, floated upon it. It was a hard, bright day, and everywhere the cool blues and greens of Lake Como met his eye. Finally, he turned to look at Delia clad only in a small wine-red bikini and a huge picture hat. Her glistening skin had once more become a tawny brown. He reached out and stroked her back, a gesture as much of affection as a necessary grounding in reality.

"No," he said at last, "not bored but a little antsy. I'm not as much a sun-worshiper as you seem to be. Were you always?"

"No, actually not. As a dancer, I tried to be as pale as possible. Later at Cambridge, I coveted the required academic gray countenance. No, I think I began to take up sunbathing just to take up my time." Delia sat up and inspected her quite dark abdomen. "Wasn't much of an occupation, that."

Daniel signaled a waiter and ordered two Camparis, the drink Delia seemed to prefer at poolside. Glasses in hand he said, "What *do* you want to do, my love?"

Delia frowned. "Don't know. I wish I did. I have tried so many things and found them all wanting. It's one of the joys of my continued study with Isabel Larsen . . . her absolute devotion to dance . . . her complete ability to focus on this one thing only. I keep hoping that some of that will rub off on me. Perhaps some of it has already. I find my attention is truly engaged in investigating Magda's murder . . . and you."

"You could make a career of that, you know." Delia looked up, startled. Daniel gave her knee a pat. "Investigation, I mean, although the other might be nice, too."

Delia shook her head. "I don't know, Daniel. Sometimes it all seems so muddled about Magda. I feel like a juggler trying to keep several glass balls in the air. Ned, Patrick, Jason. I'm afraid that I'm in over my head."

"Sometimes," Daniel said carefully, "in important things, that's the only way to be."

Delia met his gaze and then shrugged. "It's safer under the sun."

" 'I have seen all the works that are done under

the sun,' " he recited, " 'And behold all is vanity and vexation of spirit.' "

"My, my," she said admiringly, "how you talk."

"The fruit of a thorough Jewish education," Daniel said.

Delia stood up. "Point taken. Game, set, match."

"And?"

"And I shall apply myself with vigor to what is new under the sun."

"Magda's murder?"

"Magda's murder." She paused. "And you." Daniel nodded. "Well, signore, what would you like to do today?"

"Have some lunch. Take a sailboat out on the lake."

"And so we shall. How about a turn in the gardens before we dine?"

Hand-in-hand, the two lovers, looking renewed and refreshed, walked along the winding paths through the extensive gardens of the Villa D'Este. They worked their way to the old fortifications and played a loving hide-and-seek among the ruins. If tagged, they kissed. In the grotto, they inspected and critiqued the oversized, grotesque statue of a Greek god. Finally, they sat among the lush trees and flowers and talked away the early afternoon.

Their hunger and the heat eventually drove them indoors with reluctance. *"Scusatemi, Vossignoria,"* the concierge called to Delia, *"un messaggio per Lei."* He handed Delia a note which read, "Mrs. MacPhee telephoned. Call Charlotte's at once."

Delia handed the note to Daniel and hastily calculated. Two-thirty in Italy made it eight-thirty in the morning New York time. In their suite, she quickly dialed through to Charlotte's home.

"Hello."

"Pete . . . is that you?"

"Yes, Delia."

"Dear God," she blurted out, "what's wrong?" The sense of calamity, of threat to her friend, held her like a vice.

"She's going to be okay, Delia."

"Going to be. . . ?"

"She was hit by a car last night and knocked down. Fuckin' hit and run. She was pretty lucky, though, fell against some garbage cans which broke her fall. She's got a badly sprained wrist and two cracked ribs. They taped her up in Emergency, and I took her home. Might have been worse. A lot worse."

Delia heard the catch in his voice and felt tears flooding her eyes. She swallowed hard. "May I speak with her?"

"She just fell asleep a while ago."

"All right, Pete. Will you give her a kiss from me and tell her Daniel and I are on our way home?"

"Okay, and listen, *donna,* she's going to be fine."

"Thanks. *Ciao.*" Delia replaced the phone, turned to Daniel and said, "Charlotte was struck by a car last night. Cracked wrist and ribs, is all."

"Jesus," Daniel said, running a hand through his heavy hair.

"Oh, no, no, whatever have I done?" Delia burst out.

Daniel took her hands. "Darling, hey, she'll be

all right. It was an accident. What do you mean, what have you done?"

Delia slowly shook her head, suddenly tight-lipped. She remained silent the rest of the day as the couple packed and were driven to the airport.

Daniel watched in consternation as Delia downed several whiskies, a drink she loathed, even before take-off. He took her hand as the plane ascended; it was like ice. Daniel turned Delia's face to his and found her eyes fathomless. Very gently, he stroked her hair.

"I should have gone home," she said through gritted teeth. "When I realized about the wire, I should have flown home immediately. But I thought he would . . . would only . . . never Charlotte. *Never Charlotte,*" she said, clenching her eyes tight as if to prevent the stream of tears. "I let my heart overrule my head." She gave a hollow, bitter laugh. "You'd think by now I'd have learned better than to do that."

"Never Charlotte what?" Daniel asked slowly.

"Murder," Delia said, drawing out each syllable. Then she turned her face away.

For the next several hours, Daniel watched as the tears fell from Delia's eyes. Finally, unable to bear it, he fixed his gaze on the seemingly boundless ocean beneath them.

Chapter Thirty-one

Family Connections

Charlotte Frances Maitland was sitting up in bed, looking determinedly cheerful, sipping tea. Sitting at the side of the bed, drinking black coffee, were Daniel and Pete. All eyes, however, were focused on Delia Ross-Merlani, who, like a caged lioness, was pacing the floor.

Finally, she came over to Charlotte, took her friend's hand in her own and said, "Forgive me, Charley. I got so caught up in the chase that I didn't stop to realize what might happen."

Charlotte began to speak, but Pete quickly interrupted. "What do you mean?"

"Someone tried to murder Charlotte. The same person who murdered Magda."

"What makes you so sure?" Pete asked.

Delia sat down, and something in her manner abruptly changed. Daniel noticed at once a difference in her whole mien. When she turned to face Pete Manaro, Delia did not address him as her teacher. Every hedge and hesitation was gone as she assumed her place among the ranks of the professionals.

"Let's run through the train of events. Someone who wants Magda dead realizes she has acute intermittent porphyria. We'll call him or her 'the murderer.' The murderer procures pills from Dr. Don that look like birth control pills, but are really barbiturates which eventually cause Magda's death. The murderer thinks at this juncture that he or she is safe.

"However, Charlotte has a sudden gastric attack which makes our murderer nervous. AIP, you see, is inherited. *We* know that Charley is negative for AIP and had a bout of salmonella from tainted souvlaki. The murderer, however, *doesn't* know this. The story I put out about Charlotte's attack was purposely vague. Gastritis, perhaps."

Delia turned back to Charlotte and said, "I was hoping to alarm the murderer and therefore make him or her careless. I have had a 'hunch,' you see. There's something our murderer wants from you, Charley. I never expected, however, it would be your life."

Daniel stroked his chin with his delicate fingers and then asked, "What did you expect?"

Delia frowned. "At best, a bit of indiscretion that would tell me I was on the right road. At worst, a bit of larceny." Daniel began to speak again but was interrupted by his friend.

"I'm not so sure that this 'murderer' tried to run Charlotte down," Pete said, not without some edge

261

in his voice. "There are dozens of hit and run accidents every day. Somehow it doesn't fit. The porphyria bit was so complicated, and this is so simple. Too simple. It doesn't add up."

Delia's eyes narrowed. "I think that's exactly what our murderer is counting on. Oh, he's a cunning devil. But frightened . . . yes . . . frightened . . . and running scared. I didn't realize just how frightened he would become. So before Charlotte's AIP was diagnosed—and the family connection just might tip the doctors off this time—and someone reconsidered and perhaps investigated what happened to Magda, he had to get rid of Charlotte. First he gets me out of the way. . . ."

"You?" Pete asked.

"Yes. I received a phony telegram—supposed to be from my father, but it wasn't."

Suddenly Delia whirled back on her friend. "Charley, think carefully . . . who could have known of Papa's royal summonses?"

" 'Papa's royal summonses'?" Pete asked.

"Yes," Delia said, coloring just a bit. "It's my father's means of communicating with me. He has a wire sent to me with directions to join him wherever. Magda named them 'royal summonses' when we were girls."

"Quite a guy your dad," Pete said dryly.

"You don't know the half of it," Delia replied ruefully. She turned back to Charlotte, who had an intense frown on her face. There was nothing childlike in her countenance now.

"Let's see—well, Ned knew of course and oh,

yes, Mrs. Hennessey. Remember that Thanksgiving you and I went to Whitinsville and Mrs. Mac rang up from London to say your papa had wired? Magda took the message and said, '*Cor-del-ia*, King Lear has sent a royal summons.' And so she explained what the name meant."

"Yes," Delia said softly. "Mags and I joked that I was more 'the Fool' than daughter for going." She paused and shrugged away the painful memory. "And Jason?"

"I don't know. I don't imagine so. I can't recollect ever mentioning it to him."

"Do you still have the telegram?" Pete asked.

"Yes—can we trace it?" Pete noted the "we" and nodded. "Good," Delia went on, "I think we'd best provide protection for Charlotte. But not so our murderer knows."

"Right," Pete said, "can do. And I think it's time, Delia, that you told me everything you know." She nodded in return.

"I just had an idea," Daniel broke in. "Linda gets back to the States tomorrow. Instead of staying with my parents, she could stay with Charlotte and kind of keep an eye on things. Keep it in the family. She can pretend to be an old friend of Charlotte's but in no way connected with Delia. I think it would be better if you weren't so visible, Delia. Our murderer might begin to think *you're* too much of an obstacle and try something nice and simple to get rid of you as well."

"I can take care of myself," Delia snapped. "I don't need you to—"

"Hey, kids, can we stick to one problem at a time?" Pete said, sensing danger and trying to avert a conflict. A charged silence between the lovers was the only answer to his question.

Finally Delia said, "Would Linda do it?"

"Oh, yes," Daniel replied. "She'll be pleased as Punch to get in on anything exciting. Besides, the psychological aspects of this case will thrill her."

A flush rose to Pete's face then, and Charlotte covered his hand with her own. "I don't want to make Pete uncomfortable," she said quietly to Delia and Daniel.

"It's okay, honey," Pete said. "It's a good idea. There'll be cops watching you, of course, but having someone stay with you will be an added safety. I just don't want it to make *you* uncomfortable."

"No, Pete," Charlotte said. "I should like to know Linda. And as Daniel said, 'Keep it in the family.' " Charlotte and Pete exchanged a look of complete understanding which made Delia's heart leap with happiness.

"Okay, if Linda will do it. We'll trace the wire, put a guard on Charlotte and then what?" Pete turned to Delia.

"I have an idea," Delia said, "but give me a couple of days to let it jell. In the meantime, Charlotte can get her strength back." She turned to her friend. "I think, my darling, that in order to catch our murderer, we will need a sacrificial lamb. Are you willing?"

A look came into Charlotte Maitland's eyes then that Delia had not seen in more than a dozen years, although she well remembered that expression of absolute fortitude. A horse had thrown Delia and then run off while the two young women were out riding on the North Downs. Just before losing consciousness, Delia had seen Charlotte's face set in determination. Somehow, the smaller woman had gotten Delia's inert body onto the remaining mount and taken her to the nearest hospital.

"I will do whatever is necessary to catch Magda's murderer," Charlotte said.

"Good. For now, you can work at getting well," Delia explained, patting Charlotte's hand, "in case you should just *happen* to get sick again."

Chapter Thirty-two

Safekeeping

Delia watched as British Airways Flight 175 landed at Kennedy International Airport. As the jumbo jet taxied into the terminal, she tucked stray wisps back up into her chignon and smoothed out her Basile skirt. Then she walked slowly down the long ramp to meet Linda Elliot.

Not without some trepidation had Delia "volunteered" to pick up Daniel's sister at the airport today and explain the proposed plan. In spite of her talk with Daniel the previous night, Delia still wondered at Linda's role in this little drama she was preparing.

"What makes you so sure," Delia had asked Daniel, "that Linda won't find the situation . . . well . . . awkward to say the least."

"Because I know she isn't in love with Pete, and Pete isn't in love with her anymore."

"I was never in love with Theo, but I certainly would not want to live with his second wife."

266

"Oh, has he remarried? What's she like?"

"Daniel, that's scarcely the issue at hand. How would you feel about seeing Robin's lover?"

"As a matter of fact I have. She married my brother-in-law Steve's brother. We're all one big happy family."

"Oh, bloody hell. That's truly dreadful. Simply too civilized for me."

"Yes, it probably is," Daniel said with a laugh. "Passionate Italian peasant that you are."

"Well, what about Pete Manaro, then?"

"I think Pete's in love with Charlotte. But he's a cop first and foremost. He'll do what's best for the case. You can't stay with Charlotte, and at this stage, someone has to. Linda is a good choice. We all trust her, especially Pete."

"And you believe Linda will acquiesce?"

"If it's properly presented," Daniel had said with a pointed look.

"Ah, yes. And that task falls to me."

"It's your investigation."

"So it is," Delia had murmured, not without considerable satisfaction.

When Linda Elliot emerged from the hurly-burly of Kennedy's Customs she looked, Delia noted with a smile to herself, completely at ease. She was wearing what Delia could only catalogue as yet another nondescript suit and shirt, and had an airlines bag slung over one shoulder. She looked up, pleasantly startled at the sound of Delia's voice hailing her.

267

"I'm the welcoming committee," Delia said, warmly embracing the other.

"Good, I'm real glad to see you." In an instant, Mr. MacPhee appeared, and Linda's baggage was smoothly retrieved and put into the waiting Mercedes. The two women seated themselves inside and exchanged news as the car maneuvered its way out of Kennedy Airport into the traffic on the Van Wyck Expressway.

"I wouldn't mind living in this car the rest of my life," Linda said, looking around with approval, "but where exactly are we going? I think I'm expected at my parents'."

"Not quite," Delia replied. "Daniel called them and said you'd be visiting with him for a while."

"Sounds terrific. I love staying at his place. And it will give you and me a real chance to visit."

"Well, that's not quite it either," Delia said. Suddenly Delia realized how unsure she really did feel about asking Linda Elliot to safeguard her ex-lover's new love.

Linda broke in on Delia's thoughts and said, "How about you just give it to me straight, Delia."

Delia gave a deep sigh of relief; tact, she saw, would be unnecessary with this newest of her friends. Quickly then, she filled Linda in on all the salient points of Magda Hennessey's case, including Pete and Charlotte's relationship.

Finally she explained, "When Pete tried to

268

trace the telegram sent to me, he found it originated from a New York office. That convinced him at last that someone indeed is trying to kill Charlotte."

"Sounds quite exciting," Linda said. "You, Danny, and Manaro have certainly been pleasantly diverted this summer. Now, who am I supposed to be?"

"Linda Lansky—that is your mother's maiden name, isn't it?—a colleague of Charlotte's from her teaching days in London."

"Okay," Linda said, "can do."

This last phrase instantly brought the image of Pete Manaro to mind, and once again Delia felt uneasy. "I'd better flesh out your 'character' a bit. You're apt to run into some of the Hennesseys and Jason."

"Tell me something about Charlotte, too."

"Charley. All of her intimates invariably call her Charley."

"Does Pete?"

"No." Delia heard the sharpness in her own voice.

Linda looked hard at Delia. "This is awkward for you, isn't it? Charlotte is your most beloved friend. Well, put your mind at rest. Manaro and I called it quits when we were still kiddies. I'm no threat to Charlotte's happiness. No competition. Danny and Pete know that or they wouldn't have suggested me as watchdog. I'm kind of flattered in a way. First, to be included in the case. And second, to be entrusted with the care of someone whom so many people love."

Something touched Delia then, something real and sure that she had previously suspected in Linda and now knew for certain: that quality of substance that she understood she valued in Linda and had come to love in Daniel. "You Elliots are quite a bunch," Delia said.

When at last she left Linda and Charlotte that evening, it was with the absolute conviction that the two women would get along just fine. Delia saw that Charlotte had widened her circle now to include new caretakers who would keep her safe from harm.

For a fleeting moment, Delia actually envied her friend. She feared that Charlotte's quality of quiet vulnerability—constantly guarded against in herself—would always be beyond her means. She wished she could allow herself to find that kind of safety. Briefly, Delia gave in to the pleasure of wondering if, at last, she might. But once again, she saw circumstances required that she put that thought aside as she plunged rigorously forward in pursuit.

Chapter Thirty-three

End of the Means

The sound of sirens broke through the hot August dawn as the ambulance carrying Charlotte Maitland rushed through the near-empty streets to the hospital. Upon a cursory examination in the Emergency Room, Dr. Helen Friedman diagnosed acute gastritis and had the young woman admitted for observation and tests. The patient was promptly installed in a private room on the third floor of New York University Medical Center. An IV of 5% glucose and normal saline was immediately started.

During the next forty-eight hours, an upper GI series was performed, a full blood and urine work-up completed. Several examinations by a number of physicians were done. A consulting surgeon was brought in and the possibility of an abdominal exploratory considered.

As the patient continued to experience severe abdominal pain, she was kept heavily sedated.

She had, however, several visitors each day for brief periods: Dr. Daniel Elliot, Delia Ross-Merlani, Pete Manaro, her brother-in-law Edward Hennessey, accompanied by his mother and brother, Linda Lansky, and Jason Howland.

On the third day of her hospitalization, it was reported that Charlotte Maitland suffered a series of seizures. Dr. Friedman immediately arranged for a CT scan to be done on the following day and prescribed 200 milligrams of phenytoin sodium IV. All incoming calls to room 306 were stopped and visitors prohibited.

The tall, red-bearded physician gave a brief nod to the nurses at the station on the third floor. Marcie Gallagher squinted her eyes at the retreating figure as he walked down the hall toward 306. "What's that doctor's name?" she asked.

Pat Dolgen, the charge nurse on the night shift, craned her neck round and caught a glimpse of the doctor in question. "I don't know. Every July there's a new crop of interns. I just about learn their names by June when the next batch arrives. He's on Dr. Friedman's service, I think."

"He didn't take the Maitland chart," Marcie observed. "Should I bring it to him?"

"No," Pat Dolgen said coolly. "Let him learn

the ropes like everybody else. I won't have my nurses rushing up and down the halls reminding young Dr. Kildare of what he's supposed to do."

The red-bearded figure softly closed the door behind him, taking care not to wake the patient in room 306. By the light of the small lamp left on next to the bed, he studied the sleeping figure of Charlotte Maitland. She looked pale, drawn, drugged.

Silently, he took out a pair of surgical gloves and pulled them on. He carefully moved the bedclothes back, exposing the IV tubing that fed into her arm vein. Then, noiseless as a cat, he withdrew a 3cc 22-gauge syringe from his white coat pocket. He pulled the plunger back, filling it completely with air. Removing the cap from the IV tube opening, he inserted the syringe and depressed the plunger. He watched as the air bubble filled the tube. Then quickly he executed this maneuver again, adding a second air bubble right in behind the first. He repeated this process several times until a significant expanse of tubing was filled with air. Then he replaced the IV cap, pocketed the syringe, turned quietly away and opened the door. In the corridor stood Delia Ross-Merlani. "Good evening, Jason," she said.

He leapt at her, but found his arms restrained

by two police officers. He glimpsed Lt. Pete Manaro and Dr. Daniel Elliot over Delia's shoulder.

Charlotte was sitting up in bed, her eyes wide with horror as they backed Jason into the room. Pete put handcuffs on the silent man, then with a handkerchief carefully removed the syringe from the prisoner's pocket and placed it in a plastic bag.

"Jason Howland, you are under arrest for the attempted murder of Charlotte Maitland. You have the right to. . . ." Jason appeared not to be listening as Pete finished reading him his rights. His eyes remained fixed on Charlotte.

Softly Delia said, "She doesn't have acute intermittent porphyria, Jason. Her first attack was an actual case of food poisoning. At that time she was tested for AIP and was negative. There's nothing wrong with her now." Here Delia held up Charlotte's arm and pointed to the IV tubing. "It's only taped on."

"Why?" Charlotte burst out.

Jason shrugged. "I thought they might figure out that you had porphyria and then ask about Magda. I'm sorry, Charlotte, but I had to make sure."

"But why did you kill Magda?" Charlotte screamed. "I thought you loved her."

Suddenly Jason's face began to crumble, and Delia saw him go pale beneath his false beard.

"I *did* love her. I do love her, totally and absolutely. And she loved *me*. She really did! And I wanted to keep her, make her mine forever. In that moment when she loved only me, I wanted to possess her always." He sobbed openly and then said, "She'll never love anyone else now, you see. Only me. *Only me*. My beautiful Magdalene is mine at last."

At a signal from Pete, the two officers led Jason away. "We've got him now, Charlotte," he said, "you're safe. He won't get away this time."

Charlotte began to weep afresh, and Delia drew the sob-wracked body to hers. "You knew!" she cried. "You *knew* it was Jason."

"Yes, Charley," Delia said softly as she pushed Charlotte's sweat-soaked curls from her face. "I knew."

"But how?"

"Because, my dear, I knew that he was 'Porphyria's Lover,' " Delia said with a sad shake of her head. She held Charlotte to her and let her friend cry, never taking her eyes from Daniel Elliot's face.

Chapter Thirty-four

A Lover's Bargain

"You see," Delia said, "he knew that Magda wouldn't stay with him forever, and he wanted finally to have all her love to himself. So as soon as he became sure of her love for him, albeit temporary, he killed her."

They were sitting in Charlotte's living room, having brandy and conducting a post mortem on the case. Charlotte still looked pale and wan, but greatly comforted by Pete's hand holding hers. Linda Elliot was seated next to her brother and Mrs. MacPhee, knitting away on Daniel's other side. Mr. MacPhee glided silently about, attending his mistress.

"So he covered his tracks," Linda said, "by wearing a false red beard?"

"Yes," Delia said.

"God, who would have thought of it?" Linda said laughing. "The villain in a false beard stalking the hapless heroine."

"Actually, he was a better actor than we imagined," Delia said grudgingly. "He consistently impersonated someone who might have been Ned or Patrick."

"Then, Jason was the one who sent the phony summons to Italy?" Charlotte asked. Delia nodded.

"How did he know about the wires from your father?" Linda asked.

"I asked him that when I visited him at county lock-up yesterday. It seems it's almost a relief to him now to talk about it all. Anyway . . . remember, Charlotte, that visit of Patrick's to New York, a year ago June, after the disastrous Easter at Whitinsville? Magda wanted to get out of her place, so the two of you came to London and stayed in my flat."

"Right, you were in Italy," Charlotte said.

"Magda was very passionately in love with Jason then. They had met only a couple of weeks before, and he begged her not to go. He said that Magda had explained to him, in that cheeky way she had, about how women were always kept on the run by their men. She said she had to leave New York and go to London to get away from one man, while her poor friend Delia had to leave London and fly off to Italy because of a *royal summons* from another. Jason asked Magda what that meant, and she told him about Papa's telegrams." Delia paused for a long moment and surveyed all those sitting around the room. Finally she said, "Jason felt quite sure no one would connect him with the murder. He loved Magda so. Seemingly, the Hennesseys had far more convincing motives for wanting Magda dead. Ned out of jealousy and Patrick out of terror of his mother . . . and perhaps revenge."

"All that hate," Charlotte murmured.

"Yes, in many ways Magda was surrounded by people filled with hate. But it was *love,* not hate, that killed her," Delia said, quietly looking down at her hands.

"A love driven to an obsession . . . an obsession that became perverted into possessiveness," Daniel said quietly, speaking for the first time. Without looking at him, Delia nodded briefly.

"What tipped you off to Jason?" Pete asked in the silence that followed.

Delia twirled some stray strands of her hair. "Magda."

"Magda?" Pete said, and his tough face looked startled.

"Yes. Ever since her death, I've been hearing her voice over and over reciting lines of poetry."

"She always did that," Charlotte said, her voice catching a bit. Pete put his arm round her as Mrs. MacPhee shook her head sadly.

"It was as if she were trying to tell me something, make me see something."

"A voice from the grave?" Linda asked with a hint of an incredulous smile.

278

"No, no, nothing like that," Delia said. "No, just a vague sense . . . a connection, if you will, something I felt. Something Magda had known, something fundamental about herself and . . . also about me. This was what I set out to learn . . . to investigate really."

"And did you find it out?" Daniel asked softly.

"Yes," Delia said, looking up at him at last. "It was indeed in the poetry." She got up and took down the volume of *The Victorian Poets,* now a part of Charlotte's library with the other poetry books that had been her sister's. "This book was a present from Magda to Jason. You took it by mistake, Charley, when you collected Magda's things from his flat."

Charlotte looked up in surprise. "Oh, no. It wasn't a mistake. I remember taking it. I found it in the night table drawer next to the bed and assumed it belonged to Magda. I hastily packed it up because I was so very anxious to spare Jason the pain of seeing her things."

"This was the 'bait' I held out to him when I put out that account of Charley's gastritis. I knew he was frantic to get the book back. I thought if I made him nervous enough he would get careless and simply steal it. That's why he took up with you, Charley, in the first place. He explained to me that he had hoped to become your lover. That would have given him an opportunity to reappropriate the book without your noticing. He really didn't want to hurt you, Charley. In fact, he said he had become very attracted to you and wanted you very much."

Charlotte blushed at everyone's fond gaze. "Why didn't he just ask for the book? I would have given it to him."

"He was too frightened," Delia said. "He didn't want to call attention to the book in case you chanced to look at it then. The request seems simple to you, but with his guilty knowledge of what it contained, the risk seemed too great. This book, you see, holds the key to Magda's murder." Then in an altered voice Delia recited, " 'But they whose guilt within their bosoms lie,/ Imagine every eye beholds their blame.' " She and Charlotte exchanged glances of recognition as each heard the sounds of Magda's tones echoing within the stillness of the room.

"Then, it was Jason trying to get that book back who was in here that day—who struck you on the head, Miss Delia?" Mrs. MacPhee asked.

"Oh, no," Delia said. "No, I'm pretty certain that was Ned. He has keys to this place, Magda's old set. He keeps coming back here, prowling around, looking for something else . . . Magda's wedding band, I imagine."

"Well, why the hell didn't he just ask for it?" Pete broke in. "There's no guilty knowledge in *him*."

Delia and Charlotte again exchanged knowing looks. Quietly, Charlotte explained, "Ned wouldn't do that. He'd be too embarrassed to show how deeply he felt, even to me. He's a proud, hard man."

Delia sat down again and turned now to a page in the book. "When Magda gave this to Jason, she marked off some of her favorite poems. You can see the notes in her hand. One of them, 'Porphyria's Lover' by Robert Browning, was a particular favorite. Next to it, Magda wrote, 'Take care, *mon cher.*' Jason read the poem, of course, and became quite intrigued by it. He didn't know the word 'porphyria,' so he had to look it up. He explained to me that he felt rather insecure around Magda and her crowd. Magda and . . . well all of us bandy Greek and Latin about all the time. It's practically second nature. But Jason always felt uneasy about his lack of credentials. So he always looked up any word that he didn't know so that he wouldn't seem a fool in front of Magda.

"When he looked up the word 'porphyria,' Jason found a reference to the disorder and to King George III. So then, he glanced through Ned's dissertation—which Magda had, of course—and something struck him as familiar. Moved now by more than just the poem, he read up on acute intermittent porphyria. One day, he saw Magda have one of her 'blackouts'—a seizure. Then he remembered that

Magda had had a dreadful episode of terrible pain after her impacted wisdom teeth were removed. He managed to get Magda to tell him, in just the course of conversation, that pentothal was used as the anesthetic."

"Sodium pentothal is a barbiturate," Daniel put in quietly. "It often induces porphyria attacks after administration."

"Jason put two and two together, correctly diagnosed Magda's illness and decided to use it to kill her."

"The diagnosis seems so simple, once you think of porphyria," Daniel said with a rueful grin. Pete nodded.

"If the murder and means were discovered," Delia continued, "Jason believed the blame would fall to Ned or Patrick, both of whom had strong motives and ready knowledge of the disease. So the poem gave him a method of murder as well as the justification for it." And now Delia began to read the poem aloud:

"'. . . at last I knew
Porphyria worshipped me; surprise
Made my heart swell,
And still it grew
While I debated what to do.
That moment she was mine, mine, fair,
Perfectly pure and good: I found
A thing to do, and all her hair

In one long yellow string I wound
Three times her throat around,
And strangled her.' "

Delia briefly paused and then said, "The next
two lines are underscored in Magda's hand."

" 'That all it scorned at once is fled,
And I, its love, am gained instead!' "

Then Delia looked up at Daniel and, seemingly heedless of the others, spoke directly to
him. "Jason wanted to possess Magda's love at
any price. Even if it cost him her life." She
paused, and when she spoke again there was no
question of the finality in her voice. "What
Magda knew, and I learned, is that for some, it
is simply too much to pay."

Daniel returned Delia's look, and in the brief
silence that preceded Charlotte's next question,
he watched as she quietly and carefully closed
the book.

Epilogue

Delia bent forward and snipped the stem of the heavy, pink rose. It was one of her favorite roses, and this was, she knew, one of the last blossoms of the season. Already she could feel the change in the air that presaged fall. And that made Delia covet its rich pink bloom and heady scent all the more.

After finally tying up all the loose ends of Magdalene Maitland Hennessey's life and death at Charlotte's that afternoon, Delia had abruptly given the MacPhees directions to pack. That night they had boarded a flight to London and then had driven straight down to Rosemuir. To Daniel, she had said not a word. Here, among Adela's prize-winning damask roses, she had walked for several days, trying to compose a letter to her lover—thus far, without success.

Now her basket tucked on her arm, Delia walked slowly over to the old-fashioned gazebo and sat down. Her hair, hanging loose, blew in the still warm winds as she sat thinking. She held one of the beautiful blooms up to her nose and deeply inhaled its sweet perfume. Gazing over the pink petals, she imagined she beheld Magdalene's countenance one last time. The exquisite lips curved into one of those rare, self-mocking smiles of delight as the image murmured,

> " 'Gather the rose of love,
>   whilest yet is time,
> Whilest loving thou mayst
>   loved be with equal crime.' "

The poem, however, went unfinished. The vision suddenly blurred before Delia's eyes, and she knew she would hear her friend's voice no more. Then, in her heart of hearts, Delia parted company from her friend and fellow traveler. Seeing her own way clear at last, she recognized which path she must now take.

The snap of a twig brought her back to the present time and place. Delia looked up to see Daniel Elliot advancing across the park. He walked straight to her, his hand outstretched.

"I wanted to give you these," he said, as he held out a set of keys. "Come and play the harpsichord whenever you like; I bought a Dowd for you yesterday. It will always be there, Delia."

She looked down at the keys. "And that's all?"

Daniel shook his head as if at a slow-witted child. "Remember I said I didn't know what I wanted? That when I did, I would tell you?" Delia nodded, remembering their first breakfast of left-over caviar and love. At her glance, Daniel went on. "I now know what I want."

"I can't offer everything; it's simply not in my nature," Delia said.

"I'll take that, nature and all," Daniel said.

"No strings. No promises."

"No strings. No promises," he said, gravely accepting her offer.

Delia let her gaze sweep the expanse that made up the downs and hills that surrounded her mother's estate. And, after what felt like a lifetime of reflection all in a moment, she turned back to him and said, "I love you, Daniel."

"*That*," Daniel Elliot answered, "is what I want."

Delia looked once again at the keys in his outstretched hand. And crossing a distance that seemed wider than any she had ever known, Delia put out her hand to meet his.